REVENGE
OF BLOOD

"I'm Deke Larson, Blood!"

Larson's horse stood there, his head drooping to the ground, standing hipshot, fagged.

Blood spurred Stepper into a slow walk toward the man and his worn-out horse. As he rode, he reached into his pocket, found the two balls of cotton. He stuffed one wad in his left ear. He then worked the other one into his right ear. He shifted the reins to his left hand. His other hand hung loose at his side, scant inches from the butt of his .44 Remington.

Larson saw what Blood did, looked at him with puzzlement spreading over his face.

"What the hell you doing?" he shouted.

Blood laughed mirthlessly.

"Cotton in my ears, son. Gun noise bothers me."

"You—you're crazy, Blood!"

Blood said nothing. He kept coming on, slow, ready if Larson went for it.

"You got me cold, Blood," Larson lied. "Wasn't my idea, that fire. My horse is nigh done in and I've not much fight in me."

"You're one of Jubal's bunch. That's enough," he said, but *Go for it you sonofabitch!* is what Blood was thinking.

GUNMAN'S CURSE

Jory Sherman

PINNACLE BOOKS **NEW YORK**

GUNMAN'S CURSE

An original Pinnacle Books edition, published for the first time anywhere.

First printing, May 1983

ISBN: 0-523-41812-4

Cover illustration by Earl Norem

Printed in the United States of America

PINNACLE BOOKS, INC.
1430 Broadway
New York, New York 10018

GUNMAN'S
CURSE

Chapter One

Little Jesse Blood stooped over to pick up another pretty stone for his growing collection. The sun struck light from the quartz embedded in the pebble, blinding him for a moment. When he looked up, a shadow had fallen across him. The light from the stone disappeared. The sun was blotted out, gone.

Four men sat their horses, looking down at Jesse in his ragged pants and dusty shirt that was unbuttoned halfway down to his waist. He wore no shoes and the bottoms of his feet were caked with the same red dust that smeared his face.

He saw the men, shivered slightly in the sudden chill from their shadows.

The men didn't smile at him.

They had whiskers on their faces. Their eyes were dark holes, shadowed, too, so that they appeared only as hollow sockets in hard faces. Their clothes were worn, dusty. They smelled of sour sweat and reeked of whisky.

"Is that his kid?" asked Monte Jubal, the leader. He was a swarthy man with a bushy black moustache. He chewed on a matchstick stuck between his teeth. The end of the sulphur match was frayed,

sodden with saliva. Pistols hung from his saddle
horn, as with those of the others. Rifles jutted out of
leather boots. All wore six-guns, tied low, in easy
reach. They sat rugged fine horses with good chests,
strong limbs; dusty horses with alkali-caked nostrils and dust-rimmed eyes.

"About the right age," affirmed Harry Mapes,
Jubal's *segundo*. Mapes was whip-thin, with a lean
pinched face and puckered lips that were perpetu-
ally drawn up by a knife scar that ran from below
his nose to his jawline.

"Same black slick hair," commented Emmett Cooper, a nervous, fidgety youth with spittle at the
corners of narrow tight lips. Shoulder-length blond
hair jutted ragged from under his battered leather
hat.

"Ask him his name," said Deke Larson, a porky
squat man with a full beard, tiny feral eyes.

"What's your name, kid?" gruffed Jubal.

"Jesse," said the boy, who was just over four
years old.

"You kin to Jack Blood?"

The boy nodded. "He's my papa. I gotta get back.
I found some silver." He held up the quartz-streaked
rock as if to appease the man asking the questions.

Larson snorted. "Thet ain't silver," he sneered.

"Yes it is!" said the boy, starting to edge away,
out from under the shadow.

"Get him!" commanded Jubal, extending an arm,
a pointing finger.

Jesse's face froze with panic. His blue eyes glinted
with sudden fear. He threw the rock at Larson, who
was swinging out of his saddle, and ran. Larson's
foot caught in the stirrup. He cursed.

Cooper laughed and dug Spanish-roweled spurs

into his bay's flanks. "I'll get the little bastard!" he yelled.

Jesse ran fast, past the cottonwoods that sprouted next to the dry creek bed down the slope, screaming, "Mama!" Tears gushed from his eyes, streamed down his face.

"Tío Carlos! Mama! Papa!" His shrieks floated shrill on the dry Arizona air, echoed in the low red-rock hills.

Cooper jerked a lariat free of the saddle ring, shook out a loop, taking his time, enjoying the game. He dropped the single strap rein over the saddle horn, began swinging his *riata,* widening the loop.

Jesse Blood, sobbing, out of breath, topped a rise, saw the adobe house and shrieked again. His mother burst from the cabin, waddling as fast as she could, hampered by a long cotton dress and apron, and the *huaraches*—woven Mexican sandals—she wore in summer. Her long braided hair, like spun gold, flopped in twin strands as she struggled to reach her son.

Carlos Avila, whom the boy called uncle, but who was not related, spit out the nail in his teeth, pushed aside the horse he was shoeing and began to run after Ginny Blood. He, too, had heard the screams and now he saw the horseman chasing little Jesse with a whirling rope. Tío Carlos gripped the blacksmith's hammer tightly in his hand.

Cooper threw the loop. It sailed gracefully through the air and dropped over the tad's shoulders. When it encircled his waist, Cooper jerked the rope. His horse, trained to take up the slack, dug in its hooves and pulled the rope taut, quartering in the opposite direction. Jesse Blood skidded on his rump, backward, and screamed in terror.

"My god! Stop it! Leave Jesse alone!" Ginny's face contorted in rage. She stumbled, got up, frantic.

The other three horsemen pounded up over the rise.

Tío Carlos chased after Cooper whose horse was still backing up. Jesse bounced along the hard earth, his wails blood-curdling cries of fright. Carlos brandished the hammer in his hand, cursed in Spanish.

Cooper clawed for his pistol.

Ginny ran toward her son, tears flooding her face.

Deke Larson jerked his Winchester from its scabbard, levered a shell in the chamber. He reined his mount to a stop, took aim before Cooper could draw his six-gun. He shot Tío Carlos in the head, leading him a foot, squeezing the trigger. The Mexican's head exploded in a cloud-spray of pink blood. He skidded face-down into the dust, his legs twitching spasmodically.

Ginny saw Tío Carlos go down. She screamed again.

Cooper drew his pistol, holstered it again quickly. Before the woman could reach her son, he rammed his spurs into his horse's flanks. The gelding bolted away, dragging the screaming boy after him. The boy turned over and over, bumped along the ground.

Jubal and Larson rode up to the woman. Jubal's horse reared. Ginny tried to escape, go after her son. Larson cut her off, laughing at the sport.

"Let me alone!" Ginny rasped.

Cooper stopped dragging the boy.

Jesse was still, his face bruised and bloodied. A lump swelled on his forehead. His tiny legs didn't move.

Ginny saw him, ran around Deke Larson's horse and shambled awkwardly to her son's side. She sobbed and began trying to pull the rope from his waist. His face was turning blue. The rope was too tight. She picked him up in her arms, began breathing into his mouth. The boy's chest heaved as he sucked in air. His eyelids fluttered open and closed. Ginny held his frail body to hers and shook with heavy sobbing.

A hand on her arm jerked her roughly to her feet.

Harry Mapes stared at the hysterical woman. Her golden hair was streaked with red dust where she had fallen. Her face was scratched from stones. Her pale blue eyes shone with a mixture of madness and fear. She was a beautiful woman, nonetheless. Her beauty was plain to see despite her anguished state. Full breasts tugged at the bodice of her cotton dress. Her ankles were slim, her hips curved, buttocks rounded.

The scar on Mapes's face flared white as he flushed a dark rose. Spittle formed at the corners of his mouth.

His whisky breath blew fetid on Ginny's face.

She cringed, shrank away from him.

Mapes tightened his grip on her arm. The blood drained away from her arm as his fingers slipped slightly, leaving gaunt marks in her flesh.

"Pretty little thang, ain't she?" grinned Deke Larson, riding up. Jubal swung down from his horse. Cooper started playing out the rope. He slid from his saddle, loosened it from the boy's waist and coiled it back up as he walked away from Jesse, his eyes on the woman. Jesse lay still, his chest moving imperceptibly, color returning to his cheeks. A trickle of blood seeped from one corner of his mouth, but no one noticed.

"Gimme her!" Jubal shoved Mapes aside, snatched both of Ginny's pigtails up in his hand.

Mapes sidestepped away, glaring.

"D—don't hurt me," Ginny pleaded. "Let me see my boy."

"Where's your man?" Jubal demanded, twisting the braids cruelly.

Pain contorted Ginny's face. Her eyes closed, opened again.

"I ast you a question, lady! Where's Jack Blood?"

"He—he'll be back any minute," Ginny lied craftily. "He'll kill you for this!"

Jubal snorted and laughed. "He ain't anywheres near. Over to Fort Huachuca, I reckon."

"Deke," he said, "you and Harry check out the house. Cooper, you look around, see if anybody else is about."

Reluctantly, the men scattered and walked off unsteadily on uncertain boot heels. Cooper looked back once, to see what Jubal was doing with the woman.

Jubal released his grip on Ginny's hair. She staggered backward a pace.

"Well, Jack done got himself set up right smart," he said. Five years I been hunting that sneaky bastard. Looks like I finally found out where he holed up with his whore. "Remember my brother, Eli Jubal? You and Jack set up Eli and he's dead all these years."

"We didn't," Ginny whimpered. "Monte Jubal, Jack didn't do no wrong. Eli was at fault. Please, let me go to my boy. He's hurt."

"In time, little lady. First, you and me got some business."

There was no mistaking his leer. Ginny Blood drew back, shrank away from him, terrified. She put her hand to her mouth. Jubal stared at the wedding ring on her finger. Sunlight sparkled in the depths of its tiny stones.

"All clear, Jubal!" shouted Mapes.

"Same here!" echoed Cooper, stalking through the stables after checking the bunkhouse where Tío Carlos had lived.

Jubal grabbed Ginny's wrist and jerked her toward the house. She screamed, knowing it would do no good. No one could hear—no one who cared.

"What're you goin' to do, Monte?" asked Mapes.

"Put the boots to his whore, that's what."

"Haw! That'll learn him!" laughed Mapes.

"Seconds!" called out Deke Larson.

"Thirds!" rapped Cooper, running up from the stables.

"Shit," said Mapes.

Jubal shoved Ginny inside the house. It was a low adobe with a sod roof. Sparsely furnished, it was neat, with homemade furniture, flowers in a clay vase, a living room, kitchen and dining area, one large bedroom, and a smaller one for Jesse. Jubal found the bedroom he wanted and pushed Ginny through the door. It was cool and dark inside.

"Don't, please," begged Ginny. "Let me go."

Jubal kicked the door shut, his boot heel slamming into the wood. The door swung to on leather hinges, rattled in the jamb. Then he lashed out at Ginny, grabbed the bodice of her dress. There was a sickening gnash of ripping cloth. He stared at her bared breast jutted out ripe as a melon from her chest. His eyes widened. His loins stirred with desire.

"Well, now," he husked, "you're right purty, little lady. The years ain't done you no harm."

"God, please. Don't." She whimpered, cringing.

Jubal grabbed her, forced heavy wet lips on hers. She tightened up. He drew back, slapped her.

Tears welled in her eyes.

He grabbed her torn dress, ripped it completely

off. He stared at the blonde patch between her legs, shielded by thin panties.

Ginny tried to cover her nakedness. She drew her hands up over her breasts, twisted her legs, pressed them close together.

Jubal dropped his pants and gunbelt.

He forced her onto the bed, pried her legs apart.

His organ swayed like a bent lance, rock-hard. He straddled her, plunged into her sheath.

Ginny screamed in stark horror.

A darkness rose up in her mind, drowned her senses.

Mercifully, she passed out as Jubal rammed deep, plundering the wife of the man he hated.

Chapter Two

Blood headed his horse east toward the Little Dragoons. He was glad he had bypassed going to Tombstone with Curly and the boys. He'd have lost two days there—at least, another day in travel. Hell, it had been tempting. They had got a good price for the herd at Fort Huachuca and after he'd paid off the boys, he still had plenty left. A saddlebag full of pretties for Ginny and Jesse, a new fry pan, an *olla* hanging from the saddlehorn so that they could have *tepache* and sip it in the heat of the day or in the cool of the Arizona evening. Ginny would be pleased. She was a good woman and she had borne him a strong son.

Jack Blood worried the hunk of Climax chewing tobacco in his mouth. A luxury he didn't indulge in around the house. But on the drive, or working cattle, it kept a man's thirst in check, took down the nerves a notch when ragging after a mossy horn or taming a contrary mustang. He was a tall, lean man. He had a shock of raven-dark hair under his Stetson, deep blue eyes, a cleft chin, wide strong shoulders.

"Pick it up, Stepper," he said to his horse. Benson was a long stretch behind him and he could see the

Dragoons against the sky. His shadow was pulling out ahead of him, getting longer as the sun dipped toward the western horizon.

Stepper was a coal-black gelding, sixteen hands high with four white stockings. He moved under a California saddle, and the blood of Arabian and Morgan breeds ran in his veins. Besides being a beauty, he was a working cow-horse, Blood's favorite among his *remuda*. He could cover forty mile a day and never show it. Good lungs and good legs, he was a solid mount, the quickest he had ever ridden or roped from, bar none.

The gelding responded to the gentle nudge of single-bit spurs touched to his flanks. The horse broke into an easy canter and Blood started whistling a tuneless ditty. The spring air was crisp and there would be frost in the high country come morning.

Blood stopped whistling when he saw them. Buzzards—circling high in the sky over his ranch.

The air took on a deeper chill, and he flipped up the collar of his light buckskin jacket.

There were a lot of buzzards. From a distance, with eyes squinted, they almost looked like a column of smoke. But there was no smoke. Only circling turkey buzzards wheeling in vertical patterns.

Blood kicked Stepper into a gallop, the *olla* bouncing so hard he had to hold it to keep it from breaking or injuring his horse.

He stopped short on the hill overlooking the ranch buildings.

It was quiet.

Something was wrong.

Dead wrong.

Two buzzards were on the ground, strutting around a large object. A cow. Or a man. A horse stood

underneath the shed, where Tío Carlos did his
shoeing. He was haltered and there was no smoke
rising from the brazier.

Blood scanned the ranch compound.

There was not a sign of life.

He reached into his shirt pocket and pulled out
two wads of cotton and put one in each ear. Then he
drew his pistol, a Remington .44. He hammered
back, aimed it at the ground. Fired one shot. Smoke
and flame belched from the long barrel of the .44.
Dirt kicked up a few yards away. Stepper held
steady.

The two buzzards on the ground flapped into the
air, lifted lazily into the sky. The flying buzzards
flared away from the sound, scattered like leaves
blown before a wind.

But no one came outside to look. Not Ginny. Not
Jesse. Not Tío Carlos.

Blood holstered the .44. He did not remove the
cottom from his ears. A sickness began to build in
his stomach. The muscles in his jaws quivered,
knotted.

Stepper moved out as Blood clucked to him, raked
his flanks gently with the knobby spurs. Blood's
eyes flickered as they moved in their sockets, scan-
ning the rolling hills, the outcroppings of red rocks.
The sun was low on the horizon now, the shadows
of the horse and man long on the reddish earth. The
chill in the air deepened. There was no breeze. It
was as if the silence itself was a muffled shriek in
his ears. He took out the wads of cotton, but it was
no different. There was a stench in the air. The
queasiness in his stomach boiled up again and he
tasted the faint acid of bile in his throat.

He rode over to Carlos Avila's body first, to con-
firm his gut feeling.

"Christ," he muttered.

The back of Tío Carlos's head was blown away. A round blue-black hole gaped in the center of his forehead. Flies and ants fought over the dried blood. The buzzards had taken out his eyes.

Blood leaned out to the side and vomited, the bile rising up in his throat with a gagging rush. He retched until his eyes watered and his stomach grew claws. Stepper shied from the vomit, sidestepping away from the stench. Blood held on to the saddlehorn, weak, helpless.

He straightened up, the sickness replaced by a steel ball in the pit of his stomach.

The ball turned ice cold, freezing his innards.

Blood knew what it was—fear.

He slid out of the saddle. Stood on wobbly legs. His knees were jelly.

"Ginny!" he screamed. "Ginny, for God's sake!"

Then he started running toward the house. Running on uneven boot heels. Running through thick mud that slowed him down when he wanted to fly. Running through airless space into a void that he could feel like a thickening in his throat.

The front door was open.

Blood raced through, afraid of what he would find.

"Ginny?"

The front room was empty. There was no answer. Blood stopped short, listened to the awful ticking of silence.

Then, a low whimper came from the back bedroom.

"Ginny?" He stalked through the doorway, down the hall. The door to their bedroom was open. He went inside, saw her in the gloom. Saw her form, felt her presence. Heard her moan. He ran to the bedside, looked down. She was holding something in her arms.

Jesse!

She was naked, shivering. Her eyes were closed. He drew open the curtains. The sunset was a raw wound in the sky. There was enough light for him to see her better. See his son staring up at him with wide, fearful eyes. Tenderly, he lifted his son in his arms. He felt light. Too light, as if something had gone out of him.

"No! Don't!" Jesse screamed when his father touched him.

"Jesse, it's me. Papa. Don't you know me, boy?"

"Papa! Some mens hurt me. I'm scared."

His father looked at him closely—his haunted eyes and quivering mouth, blood, dried and caked, at the corners. Jesse winced when Blood moved him slightly. He lifted his son's dirty shirt, saw the hideous marks on the boy's flesh. It was then that he heard the soft wheezing when the boy breathed. He touched the lad's ribs gingerly.

Jesse screamed in pain.

"I'm sorry," said his father. "Did they hit you?"

The boy shook his head and even that slight movement caused him pain.

Jack Blood laid the boy down on the bed. He was gentle, but even so, little Jesse cringed and whimpered.

"I want to see how your mother is," he told the boy.

"Mama's hurt. She's asleep."

Blood's lips tightened as he turned Ginny over, looked at her in the fading light. Her eyes were puffed, swollen with purple bruises. Her lips were smashed to a bloody pulp. An egg-sized lump distorted her cheekbone on one side of her face. There were purplish smudges on her neck.

Then he looked at her loins.

Bloody smears covered her inner thighs. Massive bruises in her flesh, yellow and purple. He saw the dried blood on the bedclothes then.

Her breasts.

The ugliest sight of all. Cigarette burns. More bruises. A nipple bit half in two, encrusted with dried blood.

Blood sat beside his wife, touched her face.

"Ginny. It's me, Jack. Ginny?"

Her eyes fluttered. Opened. A moan rattled her throat. She winced in pain.

"Jack? Is it really you?"

"What happened here?"

"I—I thought I was dead. Jesse?"

"He's here. Hurt bad. What did they do to him? He looks like a horse stepped on him."

"Rope. They roped him. Dragged him. . . ."

"Who, Ginny? Dammit, who?" He fought to control his anger. Struggled to quell the rage storming inside him. But he had to know. Had to know who had done these terrible things to his wife and son. He had to know everything.

"Jubal," she said, her voice a trembling whisper, a painful effort at speech.

"Jubal?"

A shadow passed over Blood's face. He had not heard that name in a long time. Eli Jubal had courted Ginny too. When she was Virginia Ware, back in Ellsworth, Kansas Territory. They had both been in love with Virginia. But Eli was one of a wild bunch who were sons of men who had turned outlaw after the War Between the States. Men who

inherited from their fathers and older brothers the
lust for preying on helpless people.

Eli Jubal. Memories of another time. Eli was
Blood's principal rival for the hand of Virginia Ware
in marriage. He had been content to let Ginny
make up her own mind. Jubal had, too, in the
beginning. When she made her choice, it was different. Ginny had picked him, Jack Blood. Eli had
taken it hard. So hard he had called Blood out.
Crazy. It was supposed to be a fair fight, but it
wasn't. Eli had two friends in on it. His older brother
was out of town that day. Monte Jubal. It was too
bad he hadn't been there. The fight was rigged. Eli
and two homeless drifters named McCord and Phillips braced Blood down at the cattle pens.

Jack had taken all three men out that day. And
no one had seen him do it, except Ginny. She had
been terrified.

There was so much shooting, Jack's ears had rung
for a long time afterward. It was chase and shoot
through the pens. A child's game with real bullets.
And Jack Blood had killed three men.

He was just twenty years old.

Monte Jubal claimed that Jack had started the
fight. He had a loud mouth and he said it so often
that people believed him. Virginia was shunned as
the woman who had caused it all, the woman who
was responsible for the taking of three young lives.
No one had given a damn about McCord and Phillips before that. But they ended up as poor lost boys
who had been murdered along with Eli Jubal.

Jack and Ginny had to go into hiding.

They put a price on Jack Blood's head.

He had to flee from the law in Ellsworth—and
from Monte Jubal.

Ginny and Jack were married in Fort Hays. They

moved to Dodge City, where Jesse was born. Then they had to move again and again, from place to place as his past caught up with him.

Finally, driven out of the Kansas Territory, Blood headed southwest, taking cattle from the borderlands of Texas and Mexico—strays in the barrancas—building his herd, getting a stake in country where faceless men with no names or false men lived lawless lives. Blood never changed his name, as so many others had, because he knew he wasn't guilty of murder as they said he was.

Now, after five years of running, Monte Jubal had caught up with him.

"Ginny," he said softly, leaning over her, "did he . . . did Jubal . . ."

Ginny nodded bitterly.

"He—he raped me, Jack. Then, the others."

"Who are they? What are their names?"

Her eyes widened. He saw the fury smoldering in their depths. He saw the pain of remembering in the smoke of her anger, the swirling light of hatred dancing in the pale blue seas. It was like looking into hell and up to a righteous heaven all at once. It was like looking at a woman being tortured, driven to the brink of madness, then brought to life again only to suffer a nameless horror, a horror that was as endless as eternity. As hellfire. As the sleep of death itself.

"Deke Larson, Harry Mapes, and the worst of all, Emmett Cooper." She said their names clearly, the vowels solid, the consonants crisp. "I'll never forget them. I'll never forget their ugly cruel faces. Jubal knew you were gone. Knew where you were. He planned this. Cooper roped little Jesse. He roped him and dragged him and Monte Jubal wouldn't let me go to him. They raped me, Jack, and they broke

something inside our son. They broke me. I'm
dying. . . ."

"No!" he rasped. "No!"

She reached out her hand, touched his lips.

"Don't say anything. There isn't much time. I
heard their names. I've been saying them over and
over. Damning them! Hating them! Cursing them!
Kill them, Jack. Kill everyone of them. Kill them
for me. And for Jesse!"

There was a rattle in her throat. A gasp escaped
her lips. Jack lunged for her, grabbed her shoulders. Shook her as tears burst from his eyes. He
pleaded with her, prayed for her, begged her.

But she was gone.

Ginny was gone forever.

Chapter Three

The campfire bounced flickers of orange light off the steep walls of the canyon. Shadows danced like macabre demons under the overhang of the ledge. The bottle, passed from hand to hand, swarmed with an amber light. The moon bathed the talus slopes with a pewter haze, furred the rimrock with dull silver. Stars sprinkled the blue-black sky, winking, sputtering, glaring, appearing close enough to reach out and touch, but in reality, far enough away to be in a past that no man had ever seen.

Deke Larson wiped his beard, grunted from the bowels of his swollen belly. He stared at Monte Jubal with small bead-bright eyes that wandered in and out of focus.

"That was some chunk," he slobbered. "Don't know why in hell we didn't stay fer another run at the trough."

"Yeah," said Emmett Cooper, lying away from the fire, his boots stacked atop a flat stone. "That was prime meat, Jubal."

"I reckon Monte had his reasons," said Mapes, reasserting his status as *segundo*. "Woman was done in. Like stokin' a dead fire—poker moves, but the ashes is plumb cold."

Jubal swilled deep from the bottle. Passed it to Mapes. His shadow moved under the overhang. The temperature had dropped sharply after sundown. The men had on their sheepskin coats. Whisky in their bellies, mixed with the hardtack and bacon-drenched beans. He swayed on his perch, a round cousin to a boulder that had rolled from its height on some long-ago midnight. He scratched numb fingers across the bristle that lined his face. Another hand produced a matchstick, its end frayed and wet, which he screwed into the corner of his mouth.

"I had reasons," said Jubal, his tongue thick from drink. "You heard what she said? Her bastard husband due in any time. I want the sombitch to know. I want Jack Blood to know it was me what sullied his woman. The woman that should have been my brother's wife. The bitch! The whore!"

"I thought they was a time when you wanted to kill that jasper Blood," said Deke. "On sight. And we make that long trip up here and you don't do nothin' but work over his slut."

Jubal belched, worked the match around in his mouth.

"You got it right, Deke. After he killed my brother, I wanted to blow his fuckin' head off. I wanted to jerk his nuts out by the roots and stuff 'em in his mouth. I carried that grudge a powerful long time. And then I met a man who changed my mind. Smart man."

Cooper sat up, interested. He was not as drunk as the others. Mellow, sated with food and drink, still tingling from the afternoon at the Blood rancho. Thinking of that woman's creamy thighs, the way she screamed when he shoved up inside her.

"Who was that?" Cooper asked.

Jubal tweaked his black moustache. He had never

told the story before. Maybe now was the time. See how it rode on these men, his friends.

"Feller's name was Pawnee Bob. An old mountain man I met up with in Wyoming, over to Fort Laramie. Bob had a lot of savvy. I heard tell of a man up that way that could have been Jack Blood. Had a wife, kinda quiet, fast with a gun. Ran into Pawnee Bob at a dry camp with plenty of whisky. Asked about Blood. It was him all right, but he had done rode on, time I got there. I got some likkered up, told Pawnee Bob what I aimed to do with Blood when I caught up to him. Well, he just reared back his shaggy old head and laughed fit to bust."

"How come?" asked Cooper, leaning forward, his face shimmering in the firelight.

"Pawnee Bob ups and asks me did I suffer much after brother Eli died. I tell him shore and that I had put a lot of pride in that kid and wanted him to grow up and all. So Bob, he asks me how it felt to hurt all that time and know that little Eli would never grow no more and never be a full-growed man. Well, I don't get his drift, but I allow as how I felt robbed by this Blood bastard and I aimed to kill him same as he killed Eli."

"Well, what in hell's wrong with that?" blurted Deke.

"Yair, that's what I woulda done," said Mapes cautiously. "I reckon. An eye for an eye."

Jubal cocked one eye and looked at the two men as if they had lost their senses. He moved the matchstick to the front of his mouth, spewed it out into the fire. It hissed briefly and burst into flame.

"Same as I told Pawnee Bob back then—two, three years ago, afore I met you fellers. He put me straight, all right. Said the worst thing I could do was to kill Blood. Put him out of his misery. Yessir, he was some smart man, old Bob. He said that the onliest way to get even with him was to make him suffer like I done. I mean downright hard-ass suffer. He said he learned that from books he read once't. Greek stories, I think. All about sufferin' and guilt and stuff."

"That don't make any sense at all," said Cooper, a note of wonder in his voice.

"Oh, it does, boy, it does," said Jubal, warming to his audience. "Said if you hated a man, really hated him all through your bones, you didn't kill him. That was easy. And it was all over. Dead is out of pain, out of trouble. I saw some sense in that, but I said I'd rest better knowin' Blood was where my brother was, wherever that was—heaven, hell, or six feet under with the worms. And Pawnee asked how I'd feel if Eli hadn't been killed, but had just had his arms and legs tore off. Or how I'd feel if somebody put out both my eyes or cut off my balls. I said it would be pure hell, living the life of a damned cripple."

"Yeah," breathed Cooper.

"I don't see the point," said Deke impatiently.

"Well, now, Pawnee Bob explained that the whole bone of contention 'twixt my brother and Blood was Virginia. Said as how he'd seen the two and they were some stuck on one another. Said if I could not find this Blood and cut off something real important like his feet or his hands, then the best thing would be to do something to his woman and his kid. Make the bastard suffer like I suffered. Not for just a few minutes, but all the rest of his born days. And that's what we done, shore enough. I'd give a poke of gold to see Blood's face when he sees his woman all torn up, her hole all ripped and brimful of my seed. And, Cooper, you did a fair job on that kid.

He's got at least a coupla busted ribs and his guts
are mush. He won't live out the week."

Cooper whistled in frank admiration.

"You are some *hombre*," he said. "I thought we
was just havin' fun."

"We was," said Jubal, gesturing for the bottle.
Mapes handed it to him. "Thing is, we ain't done
yet. Deke, you and Harry mosey on back there
tomorry and see if Blood come back yet. Don't show
yourselfs if'n you can h'ep it and meet me and
Emmett in Tombstone soon as you find out what
Blood does. Maybe his whore will die. If she does,
he'll bury her. And the kid won't make it."

"What if he sees us?" asked Deke.

"I'd be purely disappointed," said Jubal, taking a
healthy swig from the whisky bottle. "I reckon that
would make me real mad."

"Blood has any balls, he'll come after you, Monte,"
said Mapes. "From what you told us, he don't back
down much."

"He's been runnin' from me for five years, ain't
he? Pawnee Bob said he was right smart with pistol
and knife, but he's harder to track than a mountain
goat. I think when he sees his wife like that, he'll
just suck air. Thing is, I want to know. I want to
know that bastard's sufferin'."

The bottle went around again. Emmett took a
bigger pull this time. He looked at Jubal with new-
found respect. He wanted Jubal to respect him. He
was the newest of the bunch and didn't have the
experience of the others. Jubal was well-known along
the owlhoot trail. It was a lucky day for him when
he met Jubal. They had lived well, without working
too hard or getting the law on them. They'd rustled
a few cattle here and there, rolled drunks, held up a
stage when it wasn't too dangerous, ran a few horses

off ranches and sold them to buyers who didn't care much about brands and bills of sale. It was a good life, with hardly any responsibility. They always had plenty of money and Jubal generally had a pretty good idea where the next dollar was coming from. This had been a side trip. A favor to Jubal. He just wished he had known about Pawnee Bob before they had put the boots to Blood's woman.

"We'll ride back in the mornin'," Harry told Jubal. "Early. Deke, you better hold back on the tanglefoot, else you'll ride with a head too big for your sombrero."

"Yair," drawled Deke. "We get to Tombstone we can rustle up some whisky that doesn't burn your asshole for a week afterwards."

Jubal stood up, stretched. His shadow loomed large on the rock wall. Cooper threw another stick on the fire. He was wide awake, didn't want the talk to stop.

"How come you don't go back yourself to see how this Blood feller takes up the slack on the rope you left him?" Cooper asked him.

Jubal sat down, started pulling on his boot heel. Harry and Deke laid out their bedrools, up against the wall that reflected the heat from the fire. They seemed disinterested in hearing any more talk. Morning was not so far off that they wanted to linger.

"Emmett, you got a head on your shoulders, but you don't think too swift sometimes. Blood knows my face. He don't know Harry ner Deke from Adam. And was I you I wouldn't be too keen on Blood knowing who you was either."

"You afraid of him?"

"Shit! Afraid?"

"Was your brother fast? With a gun?"

Jubal grunted as the boot came off. His sock was grimy, sodden with sweat. He tugged it off, laid it on a rock to dry. Its smell was gamy. He got a grip on the other boot.

"Eli was some fast. Practiced all the time. But shootin' a man ain't easy. Any big animal can spook you. I 'member my first turkey. Big bird. In the woods, over the sights of a Greener the critter looked bigger'n a barn. I shook some. Then, you go after your first deer. Even bigger. And I shook like a dog shittin' peach seeds. But a man, that's the worst. I guess Eli didn't have the stomach to kill Blood by hisself. He had help, and Blood got them too."

"Maybe Blood had help."

Jubal shook his head.

"Nope. He did it by hisself. Three men shot square in the front. And each of them had burnt powder. Their barrels proved that. Smelled. So, they got their turn."

"Sounds to me like you got some respect for this Blood."

Jubal cursed the air blue and wrenched the other boot from his foot. His sock came part ways off with it. He flung it on the rock, glared at Cooper.

"I don't respect him. He still killed my brother. I think he done it dirty, but I can't prove it. Suckered him some way. You know, like pretending to give up and then shooting him. Eli might not have had much guts, but he was fast. And he was careful. That's why he got hisself help. Wrong help, though."

Jubal rubbed his dirty feet—between the toes, on top of the arch. Mapes and Larson crawled into their bedrolls, fully clothed. They didn't say good night. They were both snoring in seconds.

Cooper got his bedroll, walked back to the fire. He stared into it a long time. Jubal watched him, then yawned. The kid was thinking mighty hard. He had something in his craw. It would come out. Now or sometime. He was a good kid. Would be with seasoning. He had nerve and that counted for something. He was fast, too. Reminded him a lot of Eli. Hell, he still missed his kid brother. Maybe Cooper was somehow taking his place.

"Monte," Cooper said after a while. "What do you think this Blood will do? Will he come after us?"

Jubal frowned. He picked up a stick, roiled the fire, tossed it in. Stepping away from the fire, his face disappeared in shadow, the dark points of his moustache jutting out from his silhouette. He took off his hat, wiped the sweatband.

"He might. Hard tellin' what grief will do to a man. We hurt him, kid, hurt him bad. Man's got iron in his backbone, he'll rear up and go after what hurt him."

"I'm not afraid of him."

"Nope? You ain't never met him."

"Last time you saw him ... he was just a kid like me, wasn't he? He impress you much?"

"Back then? I didn't like him none, because he was sparkin' Eli's gal. He was on the quiet side. Hard to figger someone like that. I'd say he'll likely buck with a burr under his saddle, that one. You likely don't want to run into him. Pawnee Bob had some things to say about him."

"Oh? Like?"

"Like a man called him out at the Cheyenne Saloon. A gunny. Blood didn't back down."

"He killed him?"

"Worse. He whupped him, run him out of town. Could've killed him, though. But he run the jasper out, tail tucked 'twixt his legs."

"That don't sound like much."

"Way Pawnee Bob told it, did. Anyways, the jasper come back. Spoilin' fer a fight. Blood accommodated him."

"Huh?"

"Yep. Killed him clean the second time. Pawnee Bob said nobody bothered Blood much after that. And I guess that might make some men think a time er two 'fore tanglin' with him."

Cooper gave a low whistle.

"You think I could beat him, Monte?"

Jubal shook his head. He dug out something from his vest pocket. He held it up to the firelight. The tiny diamonds scintillated with light.

"Not 'til you're tempered some. Blood's been over the trail. 'Sides, he's got more reason to kill you than you have him. Better make sure he never finds out you were out there today."

Cooper looked hurt. His face hardened, then went slack. Jubal smiled in the shadows. He put the ring back in his vest pocket, unrolled his blankets, kicked them into position some distance from the fire.

After the two men were in their bedrolls, Cooper thought of something else to say.

"Monte. You still awake?"

"Yair."

"Meant to ask you. How come you knew that Blood wouldn't be there today?"

Jubal laughed quietly.

"I was wonderin' when someone'd ask, kid. Reason I got to go to Tombstone. Pay off a man what told me that little secret. Yessir, he done me a big favor. And it's gonna cost me only thirty dollars."

"Who?"

"A man named Curly. Curly Adams. He's Blood's *segundo*. And I knowed Curly a long, long time."

The fire crackled. Sparks flew up in the air. Emmett Cooper stared at it for several moments. Then he closed his eyes and thought about a man named Blood.

Chapter Four

Jesse looked up at his father with wide, pain-filled eyes. "It hurts," he said.

"I know, son. I have to see if those ribs'll set. This is a tight wrapping."

"I can't breathe."

"It's gonna be hard for a while."

Jack Blood finished wrapping the torn sheet around Jesse's ribs. He allowed room for him to breathe, tied the knot tight. He wished that was all there was to it. Jesse's ribs weren't the worst part of it, he knew. Something was broken inside the boy. Something serious. He didn't know enough about a person's innards to know how bad it was, but he guessed the spleen might be damaged, a kidney maybe. The boy winced every time he touched any spot on his frail body.

"Where's Mama?"

"She's asleep, Jesse."

"I wanta sleep with her."

"You can't, Jesse. That's how come I brought a bunk in here. I'm gonna sleep right close to you." He had given the boy powders, but the fever was rising every minute. He didn't like little Jesse's color either. His chest and ribs were blue-black-yellow, but his face was pale as chalk. He didn't have the heart to tell him his mother was dead. He had washed her up, put on her prettiest flannel nightgown. Touched some rouge to her cheeks, combed her hair. She lay on her bed now, her eyes closed, her hands folded across her tummy. He couldn't bear to look at her, yet he had held her hand for a long time before he realized it was cold and hard and lifeless.

He laid the boy in his bed, felt his forehead. Hot. Sweaty. He tucked a toy animal in Jesse's arms. The boy ignored his favorite sleeping companion, a squirrel he called "Rusty."

"I'm cold, Papa."

Blood drew the blankets up over the boy. Jesse hadn't eaten. The water he'd taken had come right back up, laced with blood. The boy had turned blue, choked on his own vomit. It had been touch and go for a while. That was hours ago.

Yet he wasn't tired. Something was burning deep inside him and he didn't know what it was. He was faced with a death he couldn't understand. With a sick boy he couldn't help. That was the worst part. Looking into Jesse's eyes, seeing the hurt there and feeling so helpless that he had come close to anger several times. Wanted to shout at Jesse to straighten up, get well! But he had quelled the emotion. Smothered it until it raged like a fever in his brain.

"Jesse, you sleep well. Hear?"

"I want Mama."

He'd tell him tomorrow when he buried her. Tomorrow was soon enough. No use giving the boy nightmares. He would have them anyway. Jack couldn't forget how frightened Jesse had been when he had first seen him. He thought the man with the rope was coming back to get him. He was afraid of all men now. And Jack couldn't blame him.

Which one had done that? In questioning the boy, he had tried not to guide his answers. Jesse had done pretty well, though. A young man, with long ragged blond hair had done the roping. Jesse had been sure about that. He described the others, but not so well. Just that they were older men, mean-looking men, terrible men. But he couldn't forget the younger one. Blood wouldn't forget him either.

He had four names, but the only one he could put a face to was Monte Jubal. What about Harry Mapes, Deke Larson, and Emmett Cooper? Which one was the roper? Where were they headed? Dragoon? Tucson? El Paso? Las Cruces? Or north, to Santa Fe? Or Taos, maybe. There were a thousand towns, a dozen directions.

But now was not the time to think of revenge. There was a burying to do and a hurt boy to nurse.

Jack stroked his son's forehead. His mother would often sing the lad to sleep, crooning him a lullaby that she'd often made up as she went along. Another memory. Ginny had been a good mother. Better than most. Jesse worshipped her. He would miss her something fierce. They both would.

The boy ought to see a doctor, but Jack knew it would be risky to move him.

He would need someone to look after him, too. A woman. Someone to take the place of his mother.

Jack hung his head, burying it in the palms of his hands.

No one could take the place of Ginny.

And what woman did he know within twenty miles?

That was the problem with staying off the beaten

path. Of being alone. A man didn't have many neighbors. His friends were few and far between.

He looked at Jesse. The boy was asleep. Blood stood up, turned down the lamp. He would leave it lighted for a while. If the boy woke up he wouldn't be so scared. He walked to the window, opened it, so that he could hear if Jesse cried out. He had two graves to dig and he didn't want to leave that chore until morning. Besides, he needed to do something, anything, to drain off the energy flowing through his muscles. He guessed it was a combination of grief and anger. But, there was frustration there, too. Four men had ridden onto his place, killed his hired man, hurt his son, and violated his wife. Just like that.

As if they knew he was gone!

Blood took another look at Jesse, then left the room. He stalked through the empty house, passing the door to his own bedroom. It was shut. He stopped, listened, as if to hear her breathing, as if to hear her call his name. Tears stung his eyes. He wiped them quickly with a finger and thumb and tiptoed past the room, to the kitchen. Lighting a lamp with a sulphur match, adjusting the wick, he found the Arbuckle's—the coffee pot. He fished through the coffee can for the cinnamon stick. It was at the bottom. For Jesse. Arbuckle's always put a cinnamon stick in with the beans to keep them fresh. Ginny had always given Jesse the "surprise" and he was glad that it was still there. He poured beans in the grinder, turned the crank. The aroma of fresh-ground coffee was overpowering, made him miss Ginny all the more. He put the coffee and water in the pot. It was the only way he knew to make coffee.

The night air was chill. Blood rattled in the tackroom, trying to find a spade by feel. Finally, he struck a match. A pair of eyes blinked at him. Kangaroo rat. He found the tool he wanted, strode toward the knoll above the dry stream bed. High ground, safe from flash floods. And, when the waters ran, a pleasant enough spot. He marked out two plots by moonlight, etching out rectangles in the earth, and began digging. A half-hour later, despite the cool, he was barebacked. Sweat coursed down his back. Every so often, he stopped, listened for Jesse. He went to the kitchen for coffee twice. Jesse didn't stir, either time. It was quiet. A pack of coyotes yapped chromatically on a distant plateau. Another pack answered from one of the mesas. He missed the sounds of cattle, wondered if he'd ever get back to it again.

Stepper whinnied softly as Blood passed his corral two hours later.

The graves were dug. Shallow. He went to the bunkhouse, where he had taken the body of Tío Carlos. He wrapped him in his blanket. Struggled with the weight of the man. The air inside the adobe was sweet. The smell of death. He lugged the blanketed body to the far grave, lay it flat, face up.

The sound of the dirt hitting the blanket made Blood's gut tighten. He worked fast, then, shoveling the gravel over the blanket, unable to look at the wrapped body any more. It took him twenty minutes to pile large stones over the mound.

"*Adiós,* Carlos," he said when he was finished. *"Vaya con Dios, amigo."*

And that was the only prayer he could say for a man who had been a friend, a companion, part of the family. Jesse had loved him. So had Ginny. But

Jesse had never mentioned Tío Carlos this night.
Perhaps he didn't want to know the truth. Or knew
it and didn't want to say it aloud and make it so.

Blood put his shirt back on and walked back to
the tack room. The night was growing colder and
the forbidding silhouettes of the Little Dragoons
stood out against the velvet star-speckled sky. It
had taken him a long time to find such a valley and
now it was spoiled, ruined by men who had taken
the only thing of value from him. Jubal had carried
a grudge a long time—but the men with him were
strangers. He didn't know any of them. Their names
were unfamiliar. He had known Jubal was following him all these years. Now he regretted that he
hadn't stayed long enough in one place to face him
down. If he had killed him, maybe Ginny would be
alive now. Yet he had hoped that Jubal would give
it up, would come to realize that Eli had been wrong.
Some men couldn't see the truth even when it stared
them in the face. Eli was that way. Ginny never
loved him. She liked him, but he had lost fair and
square. Had he taken the loss like a man, he might
be alive today, with another woman just as fair as
Ginny, just as good. At least with someone who
loved him and someone he could love, as well.

Blood shook his head. There was no explaining
such things. If he'd killed Monte Jubal, too, then
people would have said he had killed Eli unfairly.
But he should have killed Monte. And now he had
to kill him. Ginny had begged him. He had promised.

He would have to find someone to care for Jesse—
if Jesse healed. Right now it was touch and go.
There was no way to know how bad his insides was
hurt. Bad enough.

Jack went back inside the house. He stood at the

door for a long time, sniffing the air, wondering where the men were now. The men who had torn his life to shreds, killed a part of him that could never be replaced. Out there somewhere in the hills? Watching the place? Gloating? Bragging about what they had done to Ginny?

Blood slammed the door, a bitter taste in his mouth.

He locked it and wished he had a dog like so many ranchers. A dog would give a warning if Jubal came back in the night. Stepper might, or the horse Tío Carlos had been shoeing, Ginny's horse, Rose.

The house was empty, silent. He drank another cup of coffee, dampened the fire in the stove.

Jesse slept fitfully. Blood undressed, lay on the bunk nearby. He stared at the dark ceiling for a long time, thinking. Jesse's breathing was audible. It was like a rasping board in a light wind. Scratching, scratching. Annoying. Frustrating.

He turned over, shut his eyes.

The sobs came then, hard and long and deep.

He let them come. Let them wash over him like a nighttide. Dark, cleansing, brutal.

In a while, he slept.

*   *   *

The men were giants.

They rode huge misshapen elephants, great bulging animals that blazed fire from their eyes, struck sparks with their hooves.

The men came at him from all directions. They shouted something he couldn't understand. They carried rifles that were as limber as whips.

Blood ran, frightened.

He slogged through the thick mire of the night-

mare, struggling to free his feet, to gather speed. A maze of twisted corrals blocked his way. He became lost. When he turned around, the elephants had disappeared. But a lone man, his face hidden in shadow, still stalked him. In his hand, a bright pistol glistened from five points, like a star. The pistol wriggled and grew into a snakelike object. A rope. It whirled over the man's head as he came closer, his arm twisting to widen the loop.

Blood saw a little boy tumbling down a dark hill.

The boy did not look like Jesse, but it was Jesse. He was calling to him from faraway.

A woman rose up out of the earth. She was light-haired. . . . It was Ginny. Her face began to melt like candlewax, until it distorted into a hideous mask. The boy continued to tumble. Now he was screaming, "Mama! Mama!"

Blood started running toward the boy. His feet left the ground and he sailed over the eerie nightscape of the dream, past twisted trees, over the man with the rope and the star-shaped pistol. He sailed on, higher and higher, trying to slow down. He flew toward a mass of light, a sky pulsing like flesh.

And, far off, he heard the boy screaming.

"Mama! Mama! Come back!"

Blood jolted awake.

He blinked off shreds of dream, shook his head. His eyes swept the room.

Jesse's bed was empty!

"Mama! Wake up!"

The screams were muffled. It took Blood a moment to get his bearings. He rubbed his eyes, jumped out of his bunk.

Jesse was in Ginny's room. Blood ran toward him, his heart squeezed, struggling in the cage of his chest.

His worst fears were realized when he saw Jesse atop his mother's bed, tears rivering down his face, shaking her.

Jesse looked at his father.

"Mama won't wake up, Papa. She—she can't hear me."

Jack took his son in his arms, held him close. The boy was shivering, his fever raging. His forehead was hot, damp. Blood squeezed his son gently, ran fingers through the boy's hair.

"It's all right, Jesse. Don't cry any more."

"What's the matter with Mama?"

Light smeared the morning sky outside the window. He looked at the boy, wondering how to tell him the truth, how to make him understand what death was, what it meant to him.

"She—she's gone, Jesse. Gone to heaven."

"Is she dead?"

Surprised, Jack swallowed hard.

"Yes, son. She's dead."

"Won't she ever come alive?"

"No."

Jesse's face clouded up. He gasped for breath as a terrible convulsion shook his tiny body. He reached out a hand for his father. The breath wouldn't come. His face purpled, then faded to a pale blue.

"Don't, Jesse!" Jack said. He shook the boy, trying to force air into his lungs. Jesse shook all over. His eyes rolled back in their sockets. Blood bubbled up in his mouth, spilled over onto his nightshirt. He gave a soft cry, shook one last time and closed his eyes.

Jack wiped the boy's mouth of blood, tried to breathe air into his lungs. He lay him down on the bed, next to his mother, and pushed on his belly. There was no response.

"Jesse," he said quietly, "I love you. I love you so goddamned much, son!"

And the tears came again as he picked the boy up in his arms, rocked him against his heaving, sob-wracked chest.

Chapter Five

Blood put the last stone on his son's grave, stood up. The sun was low in the sky, buttered behind scudding clouds. The morning haze had lifted and it was warm. That was why he had gotten the burying done early. Jesse's small grave was next to his mother's. He'd wrapped the boy in his favorite blanket, tucked his stuffed squirrel in his arms. Ginny had made that for him, sewing burlap over sawdust, buttons for eyes, hog bristles for whiskers, colored cloth for mouth and the pink insides of its ears. She had patched it more than once, stuffing fresh sawdust inside to keep its shape. Jesse would never go to sleep without Rusty in his arms.

Now the two would sleep forever.

Blood took off his hat, said a silent prayer over the graves of his wife and son.

He walked back to the house slowly, carrying his hat.

Inside, he checked his saddlebags a final time. He had searched high and low for something else—the wedding ring he had given Ginny. She always wore it. It was gold, with a small diamond.

Ammunition for the .44-.40 Winchester, the Remington .44; jerky, hardtack, coffee, a small can to cook it in; flour, beans, a skillet, sulphur matches, a hatful of grain for Stepper—he and his horse didn't need much. His bedroll lay on the kitchen table next to the saddlebags. The canteens, both of them were full.

He hefted the items, stalked through the house, his boots ringing on the hardwood floors. He had hauled lumber from Santa Fe so that Ginny wouldn't have a dirt floor like everybody else in that part of the country. His footsteps echoed hollowly in the dark, empty house. One of the men had taken Ginny's ring, he was sure. It was a memento he wished he had now.

He shut the door, walked to the stables. He turned Rose loose, saddled up Stepper. After slipping the Winchester in its scabbard, he slung canteens over the saddle horn and tied the bedroll on with thongs, aligned the saddlebags back of the cantle.

Blood glanced once more at the three graves atop the hill. Later he would come back and put crosses over them. He'd dig a post hole, creosote the wood and set them deep and get someone to carve the names in, or burn 'em in. He'd seen some markers with nails making up the letters, but these rusted out in a hurry. Nothing lasted, but at least passersby would know their names for a time and how they died. After he left, he didn't care if anyone knew or not.

He rode to the creek, up the rise, following the tracks. They were not as fresh as he would have liked, but they would give him a direction. If it didn't rain, he might track the men a long way. He looked back at the ranch. It had his heart in it, his sweat. Could he come back to it, after he had found the killers of his wife, son, and Tío Carlos? He didn't know. It was a good place, but lonesome without people to make it hum. When he saw Curly again, he'd talk about it.

He looked up at the sky. The buzzards were there, but high up over the little butte. He'd sprinkled some talc in the burial blankets, rose water in Ginny's. The worst danger was the coyotes. He'd piled up enough stones to discourage them, he thought. He didn't want to think about that. When he got to a town, he'd have to send word to Ginny's folks, the Wares, back in Ellsworth. They'd want to know. They'd probably blame him. Didn't matter. Ginny wasn't close to them. His own folks were dead.

Blood started riding again. He hitched his shoulders. Felt as if something was buried between the blades. It was a bad sign. He stopped, looked around the country. Something was wrong. Nothing he could see. Just a feeling. But a strong one. As if someone was watching him. Or following him. He turned around, looked back. He could barely see the top of the log-adobe house. He rode on, but the feeling persisted.

He found the place where the men had ridden up. Saw Jesse's small footprints in the red dust near a cedar tree. His hands grew clammy. The hairs on the back of his neck bristled. He swallowed the lump in his throat, forced himself to go on. Jesse's last hours had been terrible. A brutal thing had been done to him. No child should have to leave life in that manner—scared, hurt, confused. Blood's jaw hardened as he thought about it. He would think about it for a long time.

*   *   *

Deke Larson crawled on his belly up to the rock. He stifled a sneeze as dust rose up in the air, filled his nostrils.

Harry Mapes crawled up beside him a moment later.

The two men had circled the ranch, found a butte behind the house, about five hundred yards away. It afforded them a prime lookout. By being cautious, they could not be seen. Mapes had scouted it, set up the escape route, if it became necessary.

Both men had rifles smeared with dust to keep the sun from bouncing off the metal.

"Reckon the kid bought it, too," said Larson.

"Near as I can make out, they's three graves down there."

"Tough on a man," said Deke.

Mapes slid a plug of Climax up his side, bit off a chaw. He tucked the wad in the side of his mouth, squeezed juice, spat.

"Jubal wants it tough."

"But a little kid. . . ."

"Nits make lice."

"Yair, I reckon."

The two men watched as Blood walked down the hill from the graves, carrying his hat in his hand. They ducked low in case he looked up. He didn't.

They saw him head toward the corral.

A moment later, the black horse trotted out, began grazing on buffalo grass.

"He's turnin' out the other horse," said Deke.

Mapes squinted, saw that it was so. Blood was out of sight at that moment, in the corral.

"You know anything about this jasper?" Deke asked.

Mapes shook his head.

"Only that Jubal don't like him none."

"You hear what he was talkin' about to Cooper last evenin'?"

"Nope. Don't care. That there's a soddy down

there what runs a little cattle. He ain't nothin' you ain't seen before up in Kansas, Missoura. Home-steader. The piss of the earth."

Larson started to laugh, but checked himself. He worked his rifle out from under him, off to the side. Too much movement would give them away. While they had the advantage, Jubal didn't want them mixing in if they didn't have to. It would be easy, though, to pick Blood off from their vantage point.

"Here he comes," said Mapes.

"Be damned. Follerin' our tracks. That don't look like no soddy to me."

"Shut up, Deke."

They watched Blood ride off toward the south-west. When he looked up at the buzzards, both men froze, held their breaths. He rode on, then stopped again. For a moment, Mapes was sure he was star-ing straight at them. He looked up, saw the buz-zards circling high up in the air. He breathed a sigh of relief. He followed Blood's look back to the three graves on the hill.

"He's moving funny," Mapes said. "Like somethin's botherin' him. Look."

Blood was hesitating, looking down at the ground, then back toward the ranch.

Then he rode on.

"Not much to tell Jubal, is there?" said Deke. "He'll likely give up on the tracks. He'll lose the trail at the San Pedro."

"Ummm." Harry Mapes wasn't so sure.

"Mebbe he's thinkin' of comin' back, Deke. Let's make it mighty hard for him."

"Huh?" Deke rolled over, shaded his eyes from the sun, low in the eastern sky.

"Burn him out. So he's got nothin' to come back to. Jubal might like that." Mapes grinned.

"Yeah, he might."

"We'll give him plenty of time. Likely he's got coal oil around for the lamps. I hate soddies. Bastards stake out every damn bit of unclaimed country, think they own everything in sight."

Deke was surprised at Mapes, his bitterness. The man was a homeless rake who had been on the owlhoot so long he was beginning to see better in the dark than in the daytime. That was probably why Mapes was always keen to raise hell in every little stickwood town they ever passed through. He was wont to pick a fight everytime he saw someone wearing a pair of overalls or farmer's boots. It was something to keep in mind. He didn't know much about Mapes, nor any of the others, but you got to watching a man you rode with mighty careful, looking for clues to a past few seldom mentioned.

"Think Jubal'd want us to burn him out?" Deke asked.

"Hell, what difference does it make? He ain't comin' back. Jubal may have wanted him to suffer some, but if'n it comes to a face off, Jubal would just buy him a small plot of hard dirt."

"Yair, I reckon."

But Deke wasn't so sure. Jubal never mentioned doing anything else but finding out what the jasper was up to, how he took his grief. He reckoned that Mapes being second in command was good enough reason to follow what he said. As long as Jubal wasn't around.

"Come on, Deke, let's shinny down there and see how she burns."

There was no mistaking the glee in Mapes's voice. He scrambled to his feet, caught up his horse. He was like a kid going to see what the muskrat traps fetched up. Deke had to ride hard to catch up. They circled the butte and came pounding up to the ranchhouse in a cloud of rosy dust. Mapes hit the ground running, a strange light in his eyes. Deke swung down, too, his belly full of fluttering butter-flies. It was spooky being around an empty house, with the ghosts of its dead lingering in the dry still air.

Mapes kicked in the front door. His powerful impact split the leather of one hinge. The door hung at a crazy angle.

"Come on, Deke," he yelled. "Help me find the coal oil. We'll give 'er a good soak-down and put the match to 'er."

Deke went inside, but he didn't like it any.

Mapes was like a kid turned loose in a candy store. But Deke remembered what had happened in the house the day before. He didn't like ghosts.

"In here!" yelled Mapes. "Two jugs of coal oil and ever' damn lamp full."

Deke went in the kitchen. The fumes overpow-ered him. Mapes was slinging lamp oil in every direction.

"Jesus," Deke said. "Likely you'll go up with the house, you're not careful."

"Start breaking them lamps. In the front room, the bunk rooms. We're going to have a bonfire, sure 'nough."

The woman's bedroom didn't look the same. Draw-ers in the bureau pulled open, the doily on top mussed. The bloody bedsheets wadded up and tossed in a corner. Pillows stripped.

"Hey, Harry, take a look!" called Deke.

Mapes came in, carrying a half-empty glass jug of coal oil.

He whistled.

"Man sure as hell was a-lookin' for somethin'," he said. "You didn't take anythin', did you?"

Deke shook his head.

"Jubal took that weddin' ring of'n the woman's finger."

"Yair. Spread that lamp oil on the bed," Mapes said, pointing to the pair of hurricane lamps on the dresser. "Soak it good."

Larson took the chimneys out of the lamps, opened the fill holes and sprinkled oil on the bed, floor, and curtains. Mapes poured oil around the base of the walls, left a trail to the door. Satisfied, he went to the front room and used up the rest of the bottle. Then, he smashed the lamps and hurled them at the walls.

"Better get out in the air," Mapes told Larson. "I'm ready to toss a match on the floor and run like Billy hell."

Deke ran outside, caught up the horses. He led them some distance from the house. Horses were peculiar around fire. If they were in the barn when it was afire, it was pure hell to get them out. They'd rather stay inside and burn than leave their stalls. It was some puzzling.

He watched as Mapes stood in the doorway, fumbled for a match. He drew one out, struck it on the sole of his boot. The match flared. He tossed it inside and then stepped back a pace.

Nothing happened.

"Shit!" yelled Mapes.

He lit another match, tossed it inside the house. This time he stayed by the door and watched to see if it would catch.

Deke's mouth was dry. He looked around nervously as if to see if anyone was watching. He felt the same way he did when he was ten years old, playing with flint and tinder with some boys that lived near him in Missouri. The tinder had caught and he'd flung it into the barn. Then, he and the other boys had tried for ten minutes to find it. They'd finally given up and he'd gone off fishing with them. When they got back, the barn was gone. His pa had flayed his hide with a leather quirt and taken away his fishing pole for pretty near a year.

Fire was bad medicine as far as Deke Larson was concerned. He'd seen a forest fire once that had burned clean across the border into Arkansas. It was some beautiful at night, but seeing the charred carcasses of deer and 'coons, of snapping turtles and rabbits, squirrels, had left him in awe of any conflagration of that size. The Blood place was out in the open, not near timber, but Mapes's act was no less frightening to him.

Mapes turned and started running toward him.

"She caught!" he yelled.

Larson saw smoke billowing out the front door. Thick, white. The stench of kerosene wafted on the draft of the smoke.

Deke stared at Mapes. The transformation was astounding. Harry's face shone with an inner light. His eyes glittered like multifaceted precious stones. The look on his face was one of pure rapture, as if he'd discovered gold or been given an expensive gift. As the smoke boiled out the front door, flames danced behind the windows, bright orange tongues that flicked at the wood, the furniture—anything that would burn.

The house seemed to draw a breath and then explode as gas pockets formed. Pieces of sod and log shot up in the air. The flames rose through the holes in the roof.

"Come on, Harry!" yelled Deke. "Let's get the hell out of here!"

"Jesus! Look at her burn!" drooled Mapes.

Another muffled explosion cracked the air.

The back door blew out. A stove lid sailed through the air, whistled like a high-speed bullet.

Smoke funneled out of a half-dozen openings, spiraled upward in the air until it became one long column. When it hit the upper air currents, it fanned out, spread in a T-shape over the single spire of fumes.

Mapes couldn't move. He was rooted to the earth, gazing at the conflagration with awe and admiration.

He didn't even hear Deke yelling at him. His body shuddered as if a current had passed through him.

At the crotch of his trousers, a damp stain appeared, slowly spread across the bulge.

"Look at her," he rasped to no one. "Just look at her."

Chapter Six

Jack Blood jolted in his saddle when he heard the first explosion.

Stepper almost ran out from under him. His hindquarters dipped as he dug in with his hind hooves and skittered for ten yards before Blood could rein him in.

"Ho, boy! Steady!" he soothed.

Blood swung the animal in a half-turn, stood up in the stirrups to gaze at his backtrail.

Seconds later, a second explosion rocked the air.

Stepper backed up, nostrils flaring, eyes wide in fear.

Blood eased him forward, prodding him in the flanks with the rowelless spurs.

That's when he saw the column of smoke. His eyes narrowed, his jaw twitched as tension triggered a lone muscle.

The bottom dropped out of his stomach. The smoke could only be coming from one source. The ranch!

Jubal!

Blood sank back in the cradle of the saddle and rammed his spurs into Stepper's flanks. The horse's mane flowed in the wind as he streaked back toward the ranch. Sure-footed, he clattered over the trail, sparks flying from stones struck by his shod hooves. The animal deftly dodged stately saguaro, weaving in and out without any guidance from his rider. Cottonwoods flashed white against the deep red earth, then the green of cedars and scrub pines as man and horse raced toward the ranch just beyond the next rise.

As they crested the hill, Blood saw the house afire.

He saw something else, too.

Two men, one mounted, the other standing several yards from the house, shielding his face from the blazing heat.

Blood jerked the Winchester from its scabbard, reined in hard.

Stepper skidded to a stop. His rider levered the rifle, jacking a shell into the firing chamber.

Blood took quick aim, squeezed.

It seemed to take forever for the bullet to steam four hundred yards.

A puff of dust rose in the air just behind the man on foot. Blood saw him turn and look up at him. Then, the man started running toward the riderless horse held by the mounted man. The man on the horse drew a pistol.

Blood levered the empty casing out, heard the metallic click as the slide worked the other shell into the chamber. He swung the barrel, squeezed off a shot. High. The distance was deceptive. He was firing downhill and at an exorbitant range. The .44-.40 fried the air and he saw a chink fly out of the tackroom door just past the two men. They were both mounted now, and the running man had drawn his pistol. Orange flame and smoke belched from two pistols. Bullets whined as they spanged off rocks, whistled harmlessly off at tangents.

Not even close.

But the bastards were serious.

Blood rammed the Winchester back into its scabbard, grabbed up the reins and charged downslope. The two men emptied their pistols at him as Stepper zigzagged at Blood's command of the reins. The horse leaped the dry stream bed, started to eat up ground as the two men crammed fresh bullets into their pistols.

"Damn you, Harry, he came back!"

"Split up, Deke!" shouted Mapes. "He can only follow one of us. Whoever he goes after, the other one can take him from the rear! Now, ride!"

Blood heard them shouting to each other as the distance closed to two hundred yards. Stepper slipped on one of the sharp turns and lost ground. The men separated, riding off in opposite directions. Blood didn't know which was which, but he had two names that matched those Ginny had told him. Harry would be Harry Mapes. Deke would be Deke Larson. Where was Jubal? Cooper? From the tone of their voices and from what they said, he had a hunch Jubal was nowhere around. Cooper probably wasn't either. Why had these two come back? To burn him out? To finish the job? It didn't make sense. Jubal would have wanted to kill him personally. Instead, these two were trying to match up bullets in their guns with his hide, his name.

The two men rode fast over level ground. Stepper was winded from the long ride, showed the strain as he raced up the gentle slope rising from the stream bed. Smoke obscured Blood's vision momentarily. He listened for the sound of hoofbeats to get his bearings. All he could hear was the roar and crackle of the fire. The house was a blazing inferno, the fire fed by lamp oil and furniture. He felt the heat as he swung left.

He couldn't chase both men at once. Blood made his choice. The one who had ridden to the left would be the easiest. The direction he had taken would lead him through a series of arroyos and dry gulches, over round ground. Unless he swung back south, he would be trapped in a box canyon. If he went north, the country got worse. The man riding east would run into the mountains unless he, too, swung south.

Blood emerged from the smoke, saw the man he was after some five hundred yards ahead and pulling away. His horse was fresh, while Stepper was winded. Blood's side ached from the exertion, but he knew it would go away once he got his second wind. But Stepper would have to be eased up soon, before he foundered.

Instead of following his man on a direct course, Blood angled to the south so that the man he was chasing would have to head west or north. He stayed in plain view, making certain the man would know he was being followed. There was no trace of the other one, who had ridden east. Smoke obscured his vision in that direction. It would also help his case, since the other man couldn't see him either.

Blood eased up on Stepper. The horse slowed to a walk. His coat gleamed with sweat. He had not yet started to lather and his breathing was clear. With rest, he would be fresh in a while. There was no hurry now, anyway. Whoever Blood was following would have to hold up soon too. He had pushed his mount pretty hard. A mile at that pace would begin to tell. More than that could cause the horse to go down.

The stabbing ache in his side began to diminish, fade away. Blood took a deep breath, rocked in the saddle as Stepper found a comfortable gait. He took off his hat, wiped the sweatband. He swept a bandanna across his face, sopping up sweat. The sun was climbing now, hammering down on the land with a vengeance. If the man he was pursuing didn't have water, he was in for a hell of a day. The land ahead was dry, a maze of gullies, arroyos, blind canyons, and rugged terrain. Saguaros, each one different, studded the landscape.

Stepper shied at a Gila monster lying like a lump across the path, its forked tongue flicking in and out of its mouth. Blood gave the horse his head, let him sidestep the strange beast. Lizards blinked in the sun and a hawk floated in the distance, low, hunting. The man ahead grew smaller and smaller, but he did not turn south. Instead, he angled off northwest.

Blood cracked a grim smile.

He wondered which man he was following. It didn't make any difference. But, if he could, he wanted him alive. There were things he had to know and the man ahead could tell him, if he would.

He glanced over his shoulder. There was still no sign of the other man. But he would doubtless circle and try to get him in the back. To avoid being surprised, Blood rode behind a ridge. That would give him some advantage—for a time. He could not afford to lose sight of the man ahead for long, however. He kicked Stepper into a faster jog, swinging now to the north.

Deke Larson slowed his horse. Blood saw him stop and look back. Heat shimmered over the boiling land. Waves of light danced between the two men, hunter and prey. The distance between them was deceptive, but Blood figured his man was almost two miles ahead. A goodly piece. It would be difficult to close the gap if he gave the man and his horse much chance to rest. He had to keep the pressure on; keep the man moving toward the box canyon. From there, he would have no escape. He would have to stand and fight.

"Get on, Stepper," Blood said. The horse picked up speed.

Let the man know he's being chased, thought Blood, angling toward the rider ahead.

Larson looked back. Blood saw him slap his horse's rump with the tail ends of the reins.

"Work him to death, man," Blood said aloud. "Run him into the ground."

Blood slowed Stepper once he had his prey moving again. He stood up in the stirrups, leaned over the saddle horn and looked back toward the ranch. The sky was filled with a pall of smoke hanging over the place that once was his home. He saw no sign of the other man. It was beginning to worry him—whether the man was smart or had decided to abandon his companion. There was no telltale smudge of dust on the horizon, so the man was moving slowly, in whatever direction he was headed.

An hour slipped by. Then another. The sun beat down mercilessly. Blood's shirt stuck to his body, drenched with sweat. He tied the bandanna around his forehead, let it soak up the moisture instead of the hatband. His blue eyes squinted from the hard glare. He pulled his stetson's brim low over his face then shifted it over the back of his neck as the sun crawled higher and started dropping toward afternoon. He chewed on jerky, a chunk of hardtack. He drank a quart of water from the canteen, cooled by evaporation.

The man he tracked was less than a mile ahead. The distance lessened with each hour. Blood had not let the man stop—not to piss, to drink, to rest his horse. Nor had he stopped. Instead, he seemed made of iron. The sun only served to temper his hardness. He rested Stepper by walking him fifteen minutes out of every hour. He ran him for a quarter mile, then let him canter for another 1,300 feet or so. Then trot, then a slow gallop. Varying the speeds. Never the same sequence. Push. Drive. Move the man ahead up into what would look like a wide clean valley with plenty of room.

It would look that way, but the "valley" took a dogleg left and when the man turned there he would face a wall.

A box canyon!

Blood stopped once, filled his hat with water after he swung down out of the saddle. Stepper buried his muzzle in the water, sucked it up through smacking lips. Blood was back in the saddle again without the man ahead even knowing he had stopped. He performed the act in a shady draw that dipped below a ridge. When he reappeared, the man ahead was closer by an eighth of a mile. Blood started crowding him then, edging him toward the box canyon. It was either that or face the badlands to the south. The country was dotted with buttes, plateaus, rocks spires, cactus, lizards, rabbits, and snakes.

Freshened, Stepper responded to the new pace eagerly.

Blood started closing the gap steadily.

The man looked over his shoulder often now. Blood saw him kick his horse and rein-slap him. He got little response. The horse was tiring—pushed almost to the limit of its endurance. The heat, the miles, the lack of water were all taking their toll on man and animal. Still Blood pressed on, pushing, narrowing the distance, driving the man ahead of him over gradually flattening terrain.

Soon, Blood knew, he would have to make a stand, either by choice or necessity.

The man was smart. He hadn't tried to circle or ambush Blood. If he had, it would have been all over in a hurry. Blood knew the country. It was obvious that the man he trailed did not. He could have made a stand, but it would then have been only a matter of time, with Blood stalking, the other man held to a fixed position, unsure of where his enemy was, from what direction he would strike.

The box canyon loomed ahead. It was a natural place to ride for, and the man he trailed didn't disappoint him.

It looked like the road to freedom. The ridges started out low, then rose gradually. It appeared they would drop off again on the other side. There, a man might reason, would be a perfect spot for ambush.

Blood suppressed a grin as Larson kicked his horse toward the entrance to the canyon.

He hauled up short, drew the Winchester from its sheath. Levering a shell into the chamber, he aimed high and fired at the man riding into the canyon. The bullet might carry. It would take a hell of a drop at that yardage. It would take some seconds for the report to reach him, but the man would know he was being pressed.

A spout of dirt kicked up a hundred yards behind the man.

Blood saw him turn. The bullet struck before the sound of the cracking rifle reached him. He whacked his horse and rode deeper into the canyon—into the trap.

Blood watched him go, sheathed the Winchester,

and prodded Stepper into a rolling gallop. The distance between the two men lessened. Stepper gobbled up the yards with a long smooth stride. He was rested, full of ginger again.

He didn't want the man to get too far ahead now. He might figure things out and, once he turned the bend, he'd have a slight advantage. If he was smart, he could hop off his mount, take cover behind the outcropping of rock. He might get off a shot or two, but there was no escape. He could either be starved out or driven back against the wall, in time.

Once, when Blood looked back just before entering the canyon, he thought he saw something behind him. Or someone. It was movement. Dark and big. He strained his eyes to see better, but the shape was gone, swallowed up in the glaring sunlight, by the deep water scars in the rugged land. He rode on but knew he didn't have much time.

The other man was following him, he was sure. A long ways off, but back there—and coming on at a steady pace.

The man ahead slowed his horse.

Blood urged Stepper on. The horse picked up speed. The distance between the two men shrank.

Larson drew his rifle from its boot, sent a shot in Blood's direction.

Close enough to hear the angry whine as the bullet sizzled through the air, caromed off a rock, Blood ignored it and pressed harder. Stepper got his legs under him, racing now, the wind in his teeth, mane flying, tail straight back like a dark and ragged flag.

The man rammed his rifle back in its sheath, wheeled and started riding deeper into the canyon.

In a few minutes he would make the bend.

Then he would know.

Blood came on, relentless.

He saw the man make the turn. Blood was close enough to see his face.

Two minutes later, Blood turned into the box. He slowed Stepper. Took the turn in a walk.

The man was there, in the open. Waiting.

Blood pulled up, eyed him. No weapon showing. The man had made his choice. He knew he had been suckered.

"Which one are you?" Blood called across the two hundred yards separating the men. "Mapes or Larson?"

His words echoed in the canyon, bouncing off the walls, carrying to the high rocks, where they were swallowed up in a terrible muffling silence.

Chapter Seven

"I'm Deke Larson, Blood!"

Larson's horse stood there, his head drooping to the ground, standing hipshot, fagged.

Blood spurred Stepper into a slow walk toward the man and his worn-out horse. As he rode, he reached into his pocket, found the two balls of cotton. He stuffed one wad in his left ear. He then worked the other one into his right ear. He shifted the reins to his left hand. His other hand hung loose at his side, scant inches from the butt of his .44 Remington.

Larson saw what Blood did, looked at him with puzzlement spreading over his face.

"What the hell you doing?" he shouted.

Blood laughed mirthlessly.

"Cotton in my ears, son. Gun noise bothers me."

"You—you're crazy, Blood!"

Blood said nothing. He kept coming on, slow. Ready, if Larson went for it.

"You got me cold, Blood," Larson said. "Wasn't my idea, that fire. My horse is nigh done in and I've not much fight in me."

"You're one of Jubal's bunch. That's enough."

"Figgered so. Any chance to palaver?"

Blood knew the man was stalling for time. Waiting for Mapes to catch up, no doubt. He wouldn't if that shadow he'd seen back there was Mapes, they had a good quarter hour, maybe more, before he reached them. The bearded man sat in his saddle, a lump of heavy flesh. His clothes were sodden with sweat. Pistols hung from his saddle horn, close enough to reach. He had a pair of them, one on either side of the horse, still another on his leg. If Larson was fast enough, he might ride out a winner.

"You talk, Larson. Tell me about my wife. My little boy."

Behind his beard, Larson's face drained of color.

"I wasn't in on that," Deke lied.

Blood knew he was lying. Ginny had named their names: Jubal, Larson, Mapes, and Cooper. She was dying when she told him. She didn't just make up the names. No, Larson was trying to save his skin.

The distance was closing.

A hundred yards.

Fifty.

Go for it you sonofabitch! Blood thought.

Larson had a lot of firepower showing. Most men took a lifetime to become proficient with just one pistol. One pistol in one hand. Larson may have been the exception. He might be able to bring two into play at once. Some men could, Blood had heard. He had never seen such a man. A handgun was not much of a weapon except at very close range. And a man had to have time to aim, fire, adjust his sighting.

Forty yards. And still Blood came on.

A cool-headed man might shoot well at that range. He might even kill. Yet the odds were against such a shot. If Larson tried it, the distance would be to Blood's advantage. He could move, Larson could not, unless he left his horse. If the man went for two pistols that would eat up much time ... too much time.

Thirty-five yards.

Larson's hands rested on the pommel, palms shaped to the curve of the leather covering the wood. He might go for two pistols.

Blood watched him closely for any movement—a shift of his eyes, the flick of a hand. His blue eyes bored into the puffy slits of Larson's porcine eyes, looking for any sign that the man was going to run or fight.

Thirty yards.

Close enough to smell the sweat on the man, see the sleek hide of his horse, its head still drooping, its chest heaving, breath rasping inside. Larson didn't move. But Blood could see that the man was hunched, sitting solid, braced, feet firm in the stirrups, pushing against them. His body was rigid, shoulders relaxed and tilted slightly forward. His pistols just a split-second away in oiled holsters.

Twenty-five yards.

Larson might not even have to draw. Blood saw the cutaway holsters dripping from gunbelts slung on the saddle horn. All the man would have to do would be to hammer back and tilt the holster up, fire through the barrel hole.

Twenty yards away. Stepper sidled left at Blood's laying on of the reins. No protection from the horse any more. Coming in broadside. But it would be easier to draw and shoot. Protection be damned.

"Blood, back off. No need for you to take me on. Jubal's the one with the grudge."

Blood kept coming.

"I got a grudge too, Larson."

Larson blinked his eyes.

Fifteen yards between the two men.

A dozen.

Blood gentled Stepper to a halt.

The two men faced each other in the blazing sun, each with his own thoughts. Each with his own plan of action. Stepper snorted, raked a forefoot across the baked earth. Blood stared at his quarry, wondering what kind of man would do what he had done—rape another man's wife, torture a small boy, murder a man, and set fire to a man's home.

He fought down the bile that threatened to surge up his throat, gag him. His stomach churned with hatred. Inside, he was seething, but he appeared calm, self-possessed.

Larson's eyes were a pair of puffed slits as he stared into the sun. His lips were dry, cracked, the rivulets turning white from the salt in his system. Dried blood stuck to the hairs of his beard just below his lips. Red dust streaked his face, islands divided by the drip-lines of sweat that coursed from his hairline to his neck. Fresh sweat on his cheeks and sideburns glistened silver in the sun. His brow dripped sweat, but he made no move to wipe the droplets away.

It might be the last move he would ever make.

"You got a lot of life left," Larson said, for openers. "You can hunt down Jubal if you want, or just go on and pick up someplace else."

"What about you, Larson? Can you live with my shadow? Someone always on your trail? Better to face it now than later on."

"Look, kid, I maybe made a mistake. Ridin' with Jubal and all. Him and me are split up. He goes his way, I go mine. It's hot. I'm dog-ass tired and I got no quarrel with you, personally."

"Yair, you do, Larson. I want to see you go for it. You're pretty good with women, kids, and old men.

How do you stand up to someone who can call you, card for card?"

"Shit, Blood, I got sixty, eighty pounds on you. And a lot more gun."

"Talk is about as cheap as anything else out here, son."

Larson turned his head sideways as if to dismiss this upstart who was calling him out. It was a trick he had used to advantage before. He shrugged as if giving up the conversation, the quarrel.

Blood was not deceived.

A moment ticked by. That flick of an eyelash was as long as eternity.

Larson moved.

His hands, lightning quick, stabbed for his pistols. His body held as steady as a boulder in a wind. His eyes opened wide, flashed a quick fire. Supple hands, deceptively clumsy, grasped twin pistol butts. Twin thumbs pushed down on twin hammers. Pistols swung up, still in their holsters. Fingers curled around triggers.

Blood's hand flew like a swift's shadow to his pistol butt.

The jerk was clean, smooth as a trout leaping to an air-bound fly. He hammered back as his gun cleared the leather. The trigger squeezed came as soon as the barrel's snout had locked in on its target.

The .44 bucked in Blood's hand. A shade faster than Larson's twin blasts.

The air shattered with explosions. Smoke belched out of three pistol barrels. Hot lead fried the atmosphere. Echoes of the gunshots boomed through the canyon, faded into silence.

As soon as Blood fired, he twisted out of the saddle, landed on his feet, Stepper providing cover. Ducking under his neck, he snapped off another shot. Echoes rippled across rocky distances, bounced from walls and steep cliffs.

The first of Blood's bullets ripped into Larson's shoulder, snapping the collarbone, gouging out chunks of flesh. The man's scream followed the jolting impact of the heavy-grained bullet. Blood's second shot cleared Larson out of the saddle, buckling him at the waist as it plowed through his gut, exploding stomach, spleen, and four yards of intestines into a pulpy bloody mass.

Larson landed on his rump, his belly leaking onto his lap, the blue-black intestines coiling out in a steaming rush. The pain was so intense he couldn't cry out. His shoulders sagged, splinters of shattered bone jutting out of the skin, white as broken lilies, their stumps rusty with blood.

Jack Blood ran to him, his pistol still smoking.

He hammered back, shoved the snout under Larson's nose.

Blood looked down at the man's belly. Larson was trying to stuff the intestines back inside the hole just under his belt buckle. The stench was overpowering. Flies began to swarm.

Larson's eyes frosted over, taking on the cast of imminent death.

"You haven't got long, son," Blood told him. "I want to know two things from you. Your time gets longer as long as you talk."

"Jesus, I hurt," groaned Deke.

Blood's finger tightened on the trigger.

"You can go now," he said. "Or make your peace real quick. You're just a hair away from having no face at your funeral."

Panic flared in Larson's glazed eyes.

"God, man, help me," he rasped. "Anything—I'll tell you any damn thing!"

"Where's Jubal?" Blood asked, taking the cotton from his ears.

"Tombstone. Christ, I'm burning up. My guts're on fire."

"Who took her ring?"

"Huh?"

Blood rammed the barrel into Larson's upper lip. The man cringed in pain, shrank back. His hands came away from his belly, slimy with blood.

Larson started to slide away. Blood grabbed his collar, held him up. The man's eyes rolled out of focus. He hadn't much time. Less than either of them knew.

"The ring. My wife's ring," Blood charged. "Who took it?"

"Ring? Little ring. Pretty stones?"

Larson slipped even farther away, his eyes paling with the frozen glaze of death.

Blood shook him hard.

"Yes, Larson. The ring, dammit! Who took it?"

Larson's eyes struggled to focus. Blood saw the pupils contract, then widen.

"J—Jubal. He's got it."

Blood let him go. Larson sank back on his buttocks. Foul gases hissed from his stomach. More intestines untwined, spilling onto the earth. He coughed, then doubled over in pain as blood pumped out of the gaping hole in his shoulder.

A pair of prairie swifts darted past a saguaro, knifing through the air with dashing speed. A buzzard sailed in the distance, wafting on pinioned wings with the currents, sailing toward the two men, head swinging from side to side, keen eyes searching what his nostrils scented. It was quiet. The smell of black powder hung in the still air, thick as swamp ooze.

Larson's life ebbed away with each feeble pump of his heart.

He held up a hand to Blood.

"Cooper," he muttered. "Cooper's the one to watch. Him and Jubal. . . ."

Blood leaned down to hear what Larson was saying. The dying man made a gurgling sound. His eyes fluttered and closed. His body twitched. His sphincter muscle relaxed, and the air was fouled with the stench of draining fecal matter. Blood turned away, pinned his nose shut with thumb and forefinger.

"Stepper," he called.

The big horse perked its ears, loped over to him with a lazy gait. Blood mounted and shoved fresh shells in his pistol.

The world was ugly at that moment. He didn't like killing—for whatever reason. Or did he? Death wore a terrible face, no matter who it sought. He thought of Ginny and of Jesse, of Tío Carlos. They didn't want to die. And they died horribly. They died without justice and without reason and without sense. They died without a chance to live, to fight back, to protest. They died at the hands of brutal men. They died in the horror of mental and bodily torture. And that was the worst death of all.

Jesse's last moments were agonizing for him. A child, a boy of four summers, crushed to death like a flower trampled underfoot. Ginny's last moments, too, were clouded by pain and the horror of what the men had done to her. And Tío Carlos, a good man, trying to help, shot down like a stray cur, beheaded like a chicken with a single shattering bullet that blotted out all thought, all past, present, and future.

Why?

Blood clenched his fist, glared at the sky.

"Why!" he screamed.

Whywhywhywhywhywhywhy, the echo reverberated. *Whywhywhy. Whywhy. Why.*

The silence crowded in on him. The scent of death clogged his nostrils. He climbed slowly up in the saddle. He looked for Larson's horse, saw it grazing a few hundred yards away. He rode toward it, caught up its reins. He climbed down from Stepper, stripped the loose animal of saddle, blanket, bridle. Let it run free.

He rode out of the canyon, alert to danger. Larson's horse raced ahead, away from the stench of death.

Sunlight bounced off of something metal just ahead.

Blood slipped off to the side of Stepper, hung onto the saddle horn.

A split-second later, a thundering explosion roared into the silence.

A nearby rock trembled, shattered as the bullet struck it, caromed off with a ring-whine ricochet.

Blood raced toward the white smoke hanging in the air, hanging on plains Indian-fashion, his pistol already in his hand.

Mapes had made his play!

Chapter Eight

Dick Adams rubbed a slender hand across his bald pate. The fuzz was starting to grow back. He liked the feel of it, downy soft, stiff with stimulating electricity when he rubbed his hand across the fine hairs. He leaned against one of the porch posts of the Lone Wolf Saloon & Boarding House at the far end of Fremont Street. His pale blue eyes swept the almost deserted street. That's where the nervousness showed—in his cold almost colorless eyes.

Only twenty-four years old, some said Adams was full of tics that didn't show except when he thought no one was looking at him. And people looked at him a lot. He was striking in appearance. Not a full-grown hair on his head, an almost girllike slenderness to his frame, dark tight-fitting clothes, a height of almost six feet—he did not appear to be the average cowboy. He wore a battered Colt .45 low on his hip, the bluing gone, the barrel pitted from corrosion and use. Under his belt he carried a pocket Deringer, double-barreled. Handy, but out of sight. Some said he shaved his head because his folks had lost their hair to the Cheyenne when he was a pup. Others said he had come within an inch of being scalped by a band of Paiutes. The truth was somewhere in between. He had seen a family, like his own, slaughtered by raiding Apaches, scalped and mutilated. The shock was so great that his hair started to turn gray—at eighteen. So, a combination of fear and anxiety about looking old, had caused him to shave off his hair and keep it that way all these years.

"Curly," a voice behind him called, "the vittles is on."

Adams jumped and whirled, his pale eyes vacuous, deadly.

"You bastard, Hal, don't ever come up ahind me like that."

Hal Nevers gulped, finished tucking his shirttail in his trousers. Hal was twenty, a shock of cowlick hair jutted out from his oversized sombrero like scarecrow wheat. He had close-set eyes that were a nose shy of being crossed, a receding chin, long neck, and drooping shoulders that emphasized his long arms.

"Rube said to get you afore the steak loses its steam." Hal looked sheepishly at Curly's right hand, deadly close to the butt of the .45.

"Didn't mean to jump you," he apologized. "I'm hungry as a bear. You still lookin' fer somebody?"

Curly gave him a look of raw disgust.

"Let's get on them steaks," Adams said.

Rube Beckwith served breakfast in the saloon. It was a second-rate place, with rooms in back and upstairs. Rube didn't care who stayed there as long as they paid in advance. It had started out as an adobe cantina and he'd bought out the Mexican who owned it, added another floor and a section in the rear. He'd put in a lot of doors, a rear stairs. There was a boarding stable out back, and the men who stayed there could always find a fast way to exit if it became necessary. Rube kept some girls in a separate adobe back of the stables and the path to its door was well worn.

Hal and Curly made their way to a back room near the modest kitchen. A Mexican woman served them steaming platters of steak, corn cakes, biscuits and *juevos rancheros* smothered in *salsa casera.* They drank mugs of hot bitter coffee as they wolfed down their breakfasts. It was quiet; there were no other diners at that hour. Curly said little, but kept glancing toward the door, a muscle in his lean face, twitching every time he did so.

"Expectin' someone?" Hal asked as he mopped up the steak juices with a fluffy biscuit.

"Maybe," said Curly, leaning back to roll a quirly.

"You been jumpy as a cat in a roomful of rockin' chairs ever since yesterday."

"I got my reasons." He lit his cigarette, drew smoke into his lungs.

"You reckon Blood got back all right?"

Curly fixed the youth with a piercing look.

"Now, why would you ask that?"

Hal shrugged, swallowed a sopping chunk of biscuit. It took him a moment to chew it down so he could reply.

"No reason. I know he was anxious to get back to that purty wife of his."

Curly scowled. "Well, that's no never mind. We done our job for him and he won't be building no herd anytime soon."

"I hear tell Ringo's down to Bisbee. Curly Bill Brocius is in town, which Wyatt Earp don't like none too well. . . ."

Curly interrupted him with a sarcastic sneer in his voice.

"Well now, you're just a reg'lar gossip, ain't you,

Hal? I don't give a damn about Ringo or none of them others."

Curly's face reddened and he fought to control the flush that scorched his neck and cheeks. Hal Nevers got on his nerves. He had the irritating habit of always saying the wrong thing at the wrong time. Or bothering a man when he wanted to be alone. He was a good kid, but he didn't know which side his bread was buttered on. The truth was that Johnny Ringo was one of Curly's heros. He had tried to hook up with him and had been given the cold shoulder. Same with Curly Bill Brocius, who had laughed him down, told him to get a wig on his bald pate. The humiliation had stung and hurt deep.

The doorway darkened.

Monte Jubal filled the frame. He looked at Curly, ignoring Hal Nevers.

Curly's face went chalk. He quickly recovered his composure and started to rise from his chair.

Jubal waved him back down.

"Just rode in," he said. "Meet you out at the bar. Take your time."

Jubal turned and was gone. Curly doused the quirly in his plate.

"You get scarce, Hal," he said. "I got business."

"Ain't that—"

"Hal, don't go mixin' in." Curly tossed a cartwheel on the table, got up. "You go on and hook up with someone. Slaughter might need hands."

"Ain't we—"

"No, we ain't. You tell the others to look out for theirselfs."

With that, Curly left the room. Hal stared at him, shrugged, went back to the dregs on his plate.

Jubal was looking at a copy of the *Epitaph,* a bottle of whisky on the table, a half-full glass of Old

Overholt next to it. Curly saw that his eyes were rheumic from lack of sleep, his beard untrimmed. He couldn't have been in town long. Curly looked around the saloon to see if the other boys were there. Jubal was alone. The barkeep, husband of the cook, had the morning duty. Mostly his job was to clean up the glasses left by the night barkeep and to clean off all the shelves, polish the bar and take care of customers. Curly knew him only as Pancho. Beyond that, he didn't care much.

"Sit down, Curly," Jubal said, hissing through a matchstick stuck between his teeth.

"Anything new?" Curly asked, tentatively. He sat down.

Jubal laughed drily, worried the match to the other side of his mouth.

"You did good, Curly. I owe you. The timing was right."

"Wha—what did you do?" the bald-pated man leaned over the table, whispered.

"Whisky? This is prime. None of that Taos lightning."

"Ah, too early for me. I just finished breakfast."

"Me'n Cooper been ridin' all night. Broke fast at Benson afore dawn. Got some knots unkinked."

"Where's Deke and Harry?"

Jubal thumbed over his shoulder.

"They're a-comin'. Stayed behind to assess the damages." Jubal reached into his pocket, took out a small roll of bills. He shoved them across the table to Curly. "Here's what I owe you."

Curly didn't touch the roll. He stared at it, then at Jubal.

"Go on, take it. You earned it."

"What about Blood?"

"Oh, Deke and Harry'll be along directly. Blood's got a lot to think about, I reckon."

"Did you . . . did she . . . I mean . . ."

"You mean was his woman there? She was and she got taken care of real good. Now, there's your money, Curly. And you're in the clear."

Curly picked up the money and idly counted it. It was all there. Thirty dollars.

"I'll accept the money, but you know what I really want, Jubal."

Jubal extracted the matchstick from his mouth, finished off the glass of whisky. He closed his eyes as if savoring the heat. For a moment, Curly thought he was falling asleep in his chair. But Jubal shook his big frame and opened his eyes.

He rubbed the bridge of his nose as if in pain.

"Curly," he said finally, "you got ambition. I know you tried to get on with Johnny Ringo and that bunch. And that Bill Brocius turned you down flat. Well, I appreciate you wanting to jine up with me. And I'll give you some good advice: count yourself lucky you ain't in with that bunch, 'cause they're all one now. Earp is all family and he won't have any outsiders. The Clantons is finished, 'cept for that yellowback Ike and his no-account kin. So, that leaves only me and my bunch. At the moment, we're full up, and that's the truth."

But I can't make no money herdin' beeves! And I got a lot to learn. But how in hell can I learn it if'n nobody'll give me the chance?"

"Don't whine, Curly. I don't like whinin'."

"Sorry."

"One thing about you, is that you stand out. Let your hair grow back. Gray or black, it don't make no difference. And start wearin' ordinary clothes. If you don't like your gray hair then put some black boot polish on it and wear a big hat. Me and my bunch don't chunk no rocks in the lake. So, we don't make no ripples. We live quiet and we walk polite around the star-packers."

"I know. You're the best, Jubal. You don't have to convince me."

"This ain't no advertisement, Curly. Ever wonder why we get along? Well, if I ever take you on, I'll maybe tell you. But you got something to chaw on for a while and we'll leave it at that."

Curly started to say something but decided against it. At least Jubal had left the door open and that was something. There was still hope.

Jubal reached in his vest pocket and took out Ginny's ring. He held it to the light, squinting at its tiny sparkles.

Curly's mouth dropped open.

"Why that's . . ."

Jubal grinned.

"Pretty, ain't it?"

"I admired it a time or two. Did Miz Virginia give it to you?"

Jubal threw back his shaggy head and roared with laughter. The laugh was hollow in the almost empty room. Hal Nevers came out to see what was happening, then returned without saying anything. His boots rang on the hardwood floors as he continued past the dining room to the hall that led to his own room.

"She give me more'n that," Jubal guffawed. "A slight more."

"You didn't—"

"Now, Curly, don't fret yourself about what we did or didn't do. We done what was offered to us to do and that was that!"

Curly looked at Jubal with renewed interest. When

he had agreed to tell the outlaw that Blood would
be gone during a certain time period, he hadn't
asked why. It had something to do with an old
grudge. Yet if Jubal had gone there when Blood
was still at Fort Huachuca, then he must have done
something bad to his wife, too. Maybe to the kid, as
well. Curly wondered if he'd ever find out just what
did happen at Blood's ranch.

"What're you going to do with that—with her
ring?"

"Why? You want to buy it?"

"I might. There's a girl I'm pretty sweet on. If'n I
had a ring like that, she just might—"

"Might drop her britches for you, eh, Curly?"

Curly flushed. Jubal poured another drink. He
was about three sheets to the wind as it was, Curly
thought. Either he had drunk too much or been
without sleep too long. Or both.

"Well, she—she's a virgin, I guess."

"Haw! Shit!" Jubal slapped his ham of a leg and
roared with laughter again. "Hell, if she's a virgin,
I'll give you the damn pretty. But if she ain't, I
want fifty bucks on the barrelhead."

"I'll give you fifty for it now," Curly said, uneasy.
He didn't know whether Jubal was funning him or
not. He just felt uncomfortable.

"Hell, you got a deal, 'chacho. Fork it on over."

Curly gave Jubal the thirty dollars back and a
double eagle besides. He still had money left and
some saved up. But he didn't want to go back to
working for wages again.

Since the silver strike a couple of years before,
when Ed Schieffelin stumbled over the richest strike
in frontier history, as he was poking his pick into
the mountain slopes east of the San Pedro Valley,
everyone had money except a few hard-luck cases

like himself. It was Schieffelin who had called his staked claim "Tombstone." Since then, the town had drawn every thief and cutthroat in the West to its maw. Silver, assaying at twenty thousand dollars a ton, became the chief preoccupation of hard-luck prospectors, robbers, bankers, merchants, and gamblers. Tombstone boomed. A stageline was established between Tucson and Tombstone, bringing in freight and people. The whores came in the first flood and set up in cribs along Allen Street and a few on Fremont. Tombstone was a wide-open city and it hadn't changed much since 1878 when Schieffelin had cracked open the first vein of silver.

Jubal kissed the ring and handed it to Curly.

Pancho looked at the two curiously as he mopped the bar to a high sheen.

Curly put the ring deep inside his pocket. He grinned wide.

"Maybe I'll have that drink now," he said.

"Pancho, bring another glass," ordered Jubal.

The sound of boots clumping on the porch drew the men's attention to the door.

"Make that two glasses," Jubal said.

"Sí, señor," assented the barkeep.

A nervous young man with fresh-cut short blond hair came through the batwing doors. Spittle bubbled at the corners of his mouth. He wore new clothes that fit him loosely. On his vest, a deputy's star shone bright. His large-roweled spurs jingled as he walked toward the table.

"Uh-oh," breathed Curly.

"Set a chair," beamed Jubal. "Deputy Ed Collins, ain't it?"

The young man nodded, smiled weakly.

"Shake hands with Curly Adams, Deputy."

Deputy Collins shook Adams's hand as he sat down.

He pushed back his new Stetson, stretched out his legs adorned with kidskin half-boots.

"I just got sworn in a half-hour ago," said Collins.

"Now we're all set," said Jubal. "Blood will have a hard way to go if he comes to Tombstone."

Curly was puzzled. Something was going on he didn't understand. Jubal poured three drinks, raised his glass in a toast.

"Here's to law and order," he said.

"Yeah," said Ed Collins, who had formerly gone by the name of Emmett Cooper.

The men drank. Collins and Jubal laughed until their eyes ran with tears.

Curly felt a tightening in his gut that he couldn't explain.

Chapter Nine

Blood pulled himself back up in the saddle after the sixth shot. There was a good chance that Mapes would have to reload—unless he wanted to empty his rifle and take the chance that Blood would run him down.

Smoke hung in clusters from a clump of rocks off to the right. Blood's ears rang with the booming repercussions of the explosions. He saw Mapes scrambling down from the rocks, disappearing over the other side.

Blood drew up, shoved his pistol back in its holster. Quickly, he stuck cotton balls in both ears, drew the Winchester from its scabbard. He approached the rocks warily, cocking as he rode. A fresh shell slid into the magazine with a harsh metallic sound.

A horrible cry reached his ears, muffled. A shriek of pain that was almost human. Just ahead, in a shallow gully, he saw Larson's horse. It was down on its side, its legs sawing the air feebly. Its neck and belly ran with bright ribbons of blood, a crimson sash girdled its flanks. It had caught at least two, possibly three, bullets. The horse's eyes rolled when he rode up, and again there was that terrible

near-human bleating. Blood threw down on the animal, squeezed the shot off without thinking. The
horse's forehead twitched. Dust flew out of its hide.
It thrashed a few more times and then was still; out
of its misery.

It was hell, killing a big animal like that. But the
horse was in mortal pain and there was no reason
for it to suffer needlessly.

Besides, the horse had most likely saved Blood's
life. Running between him and the bushwacker. He
owned Larson one if they ever met up in some dark
or shining beyond. The man had been good for something, even if he had to die first.

Blood turned away. He kept seeing little Jesse's
face, the pain in his eyes. Kept hearing his screams
when his mother wouldn't wake up.

Mapes!

He must know now that Larson wasn't coming
out!

Blood raced to the rise, where he commanded a
better view. The sound of hoofbeats carried over the
dry still air. A cloud of dust rose up behind the
fleeing rider.

Blood jacked another shell into the chamber.

Took aim, led Mapes a dozen feet. Squeezed. The
rifle bucked against his shoulder. Stepper steadied
himself. Orange flame scorched the air. A cloud of
white smoke obscured Blood's vision for a few moments. The smoke just hung there, then gradually
broke up into gauzy wisps. The acrid smell of powder scratched at his nostrils.

Mapes topped a rise, then dipped out of sight,
smacking leather.

Missed!

The range was long, though, and Blood had no

time to worry over the shot. It had put some ginger under Mapes's tail and rammed it high.

Stepper, though, didn't have another good chase in him just then. Blood knew that. If he pushed him now, he might lose him. Forever. It would be better to rest him and grain him. Mapes would slow down soon. He couldn't hightail it for long. The man was a coward. A damned bushwhacker. When he knew Larson wasn't going to be in on it, he had run off instead of facing Blood down. It was still another clue to the man's dubious character.

Mapes was headed south. Bypassing Benson, he could be in Tombstone by morning if he made a dry camp somewhere along the way. Blood could press him, but it might be better to let him think he wasn't being chased. It was a good forty miles to Tombstone but if Mapes thought he had eluded his pursuer, he might slow down. It was a hard forty-mile ride. Hard as hell.

He looked at the sun, marked its progress in the afternoon sky. He measured its distance from the western horizon by holding up his hand, counting the fingers between the sun and the earth. Six fingers. Fifteen minutes, approximately, to a finger. He had a good hour and a half before sunset. He might make another ten or fifteen miles, but that was doubtful. There was still the San Pedro to cross and rough country on both sides.

He sheathed the rifle after reloading it and let Stepper have his head. When he drifted, he brought him back on the track. Mapes was not hard to follow. He had broken some brush and left iron smears on stones. The man was pushing his horse, and there was a lot of heat left in the day.

There was a possibility that Mapes might have run out of food and water. If so, he might ride for

one of the scattered ranches on the way to Benson.
There was one big spread in particular that he
would have to cross—the Cordwainers. Luke Cordwainer was known far and wide for his hospitality
to strangers. He didn't ask a lot of questions and he
had plenty of spare bunk space. Luke's wife, Roxanne, made the best bear claws in the country.
Their daughter, Celeste, was a pretty fair cook, too.
He would have sad news for them, but they had
befriended him and Ginny when they had first
started setting up the ranch. It was the least he
could do, stop by and ask if Mapes had been by, or
Jubal, and tell them what had happened. They would
want to know. Stepper could have a few hours rest,
some hay and grain.

While the light held, Blood followed Mapes's
tracks. They continued to lead south, in the general
direction of the Cordwainer spread northwest of
Dragoon.

There was evidence that the man he was tracking had slowed down. He found a place where Mapes
had alighted from his horse and relieved himself. In
another spot, he found a burnt match and traces of
tobacco. Here horse's hooves had sunk deeper into
the soft earth—a sure indication that Mapes had
probably stopped to roll a quirly. So, he didn't know
he was still being followed. Or, if he did, he figured
he was far enough ahead to stop worrying. Farther
on, Mapes had left his horse to reconnoiter atop a
jumble of rocks. So, the man was watching his
backtrail every so often. The question was: did he
know that Blood was still behind him? . . . Had he
spotted Blood from that vantage point?

There was no way to tell for sure. From the heat
of the last horse droppings, Blood figured that Mapes
probably was at least an hour ahead. Maybe more.

Maybe less. The steam had dissipated, but the droppings were still fairly warm. The heat of the day could account for some of the warmth.

A roadrunner startled Stepper as they tracked across a wide arroyo. Stepper spooked and started hunting clouds, rearing back and sawing the air with his forefeet. Blood hung on, cursing the roadrunner. He couldn't afford to fall off, risk injury. A man landing on hard earth could easily wrench his back out of place, or worse, break a leg or an arm. He steadied the animal, resolved to choke the horn a little tighter in the rough spots.

The miles flowed under Stepper's hooves as the sun dipped lower in the sky. Blood stopped to water the animal and fill his own belly. The heat sapped him of strength, sucked out the fluids of his body through the pores of his skin. The strain was beginning to tell. Ginny's and Jesse's deaths, the killing of Tío Carlos and then the gun duel with Larson—all had tapped a hidden drainhole of energy. Fatigue weighted his muscles, began to fog his vision. He stretched, stood up in the stirrups. Rubbed his eyes. Yawned.

He began to see things that weren't there. Or if there, were not what he thought they were. Tall saguaros were men, standing bold, armed, ready to blow him out of the saddle. A rock moved, resembling a crawling figure. Sunlight danced on quartz and he thought a dozen rifles were aimed at him. Sometimes his ears strained at the silence and, at others, pounded from Stepper's hooves thudding into hard ground.

He rode right on by it, without noticing.

Cursing, Blood wheeled Stepper, savagely jerking the reins. The bit cut into the horse's mouth cruelly.

But Mapes had circled.

He had almost missed it!

Damn!

Five minutes later, he picked up the track. It was true. Mapes had run out on him. He was no longer heading south, but had swung west. Now, Blood was riding straight into the sun. He cursed himself for being a fool. He had let his mind wander and now he was at a disadvantage. He pulled his hat brim low, but it did little good. If he dropped his head he wouldn't be able to see what lay ahead. If he kept it up, the sun clawed at his eyes with scorching molten fingers, blinding him to danger.

Mapes was no piker. He was plenty smart. His timing couldn't have been better.

The miles had lulled Blood into a semi-stupor. The sun was low in the sky, almost level with his eyes.

Suddenly, Blood realized that his quarry was no coward, but a dangerous man who played the odds. And now, the odds were in his favor.

Mapes, it seemed, had deliberately slowed down. The hour's distance had dwindled. To what? Minutes? Seconds?

The clam-cold moss of fear slithered into Blood's belly. His eyes narrowed, flicked over the country ahead. The land was broken by arroyos, gullies, dry washes. Land ripped by waters cascading down from the mesas, the plateaus. A flash-flood land, where a sudden storm could sweep a man to his death in seconds, without warning. A land where concealment was easy. A land where death could wait and not be seen nor heard.

Blood's scalp prickled as he slowly followed the new trail. It was painstaking work, made doubly hard by the need for caution. Mapes was being more careful now, too. The trail was more difficult to follow. Sometimes, Blood had to dismount and search for a clue on foot: an overturned stone, a hoof mark in the dust, a bent or broken twig, the scar of a shoe on stone.

A prairie chicken drummed in the distance.

Blood stopped; listened. A warning? His ears strained against the ensuing silence; he struggled to pinpoint the direction of the sounding.

A quail piped on a distant hill. *Cuh-cuh-cuh! Cuh-cuh-cuh!*

Blood twisted in the saddle, sweeping the empty land with a searching gaze.

Silence again.

Long shadows stretched out over the land, stripping it with premonitions of dusk. Thin high clouds battened the horizon with cottony rolls turning molten as the sun sank toward the far sea. Blood's nerves prickled with every sound now. A brace of prairie swifts sliced through the sky, veered off at right angles to a low hill ahead. A jack rabbit loped over the crest of a sage-dotted ridge, startled by something or someone, a quarter mile off to the right.

Blood's stomach knotted as the fear crawled in a slow ooze through his groin. He dangled his right hand near the butt of his pistol, ready to snatch it from its leather at the first flicker of unnatural, unexpected movement.

The sun held on the horizon, a shimmering molten ball wreathed by fiery clouds. The top of its circle held aloft by jutting peaks.

Stepper gave him the first warning. The horse stopped, stiffened his ears and whinnied low.

Blood clawed for his pistol. Metal whispered against leather.

An orange flower blossomed on a hillock two hundred yards to the right. White smoke puffed into the air. The crack of the bullet racketed his ears a split-second after the air sizzled inches from his head.

The skyline swallowed the sun, leaving golden-rimmed clouds framing the western sky like furled curtains waiting to fall on an empty stage.

A bullbat knifed past overhead, a tattered rag in the crepuscular silence that followed the shot.

Blood fired two futile shots from his pistol, reacting in anger and surprise. Muttering an incomplete oath, he rammed the pistol back in its leather and snatched at the butt of the Winchester.

Another shot cracked the stillness.

Blood felt a hammering blow slam into his hip. He twisted in pain, the rifle half out of its sheath. A sticky wetness crawled down his right leg. Light-headed, he worked the rifle in what seemed to him slow-motion. His hands moved like underwater birds as his vision swam with shimmering waves. A terrible weakness flooded through him. His arms turned leaden as the shock of the bullet drenched his senses. The clam-moss of fear hardened into a ball turning him sick. Bile rose up in his throat. He fought to stay himself from falling. The rifle came to his shoulder. The darkening horizon blurred as the sky began to rust and purple. Wisps of smoke hung in the air, and he pulled the trigger again and again with no effect.

The rifle wasn't cocked!

He brought it down, pushed against the lever. Slow! Too slow! The action was sluggish. He pushed on the lever and felt it give.

Stepper danced away in confusion, circled. Blood swayed, lunged an arm out, a hand to grasp the horn.

Blood gagged on the eruption in his throat.

The vomit surged up, strangling him. He sucked in particles. His air supply shut off as if someone had tripped a damper in his throat. The sky spun. The dusk churned to a smoky haze. Stepper whinnied as another shot fried the air, rang against rocks showering splintered projectiles of stone into the air. The rock slivers stung the horse's legs like primitive daggers. Stepper bolted and the rifle fell from Blood's hands.

Another shot rang out.

He screamed as the bullet caught him low in the back, ripping through the cantle.

Slowed down, the bullet twisted and tumbled as it slammed into him. A giant maul slammed into his flesh, pitching him forward over the saddle horn. Another bullet chilled his spine as it whistled between Stepper's ears.

The horse raced off at full speed, spurred by the showers of rock that stung his legs. In full gallop, Stepper flattened his ears. His tail streamed straight out from his hindquarters. His mane trailed backward, whipped by the wind of headlong flight.

Blood held on, doubled-up over the horn, waves of pain and nausea rolling through him, clouding his senses. Searing shots of purest agony rippled up his back and he didn't care. His hat blew off, and sprayed blood from his leg and back stippled it before it fell.

There were no more shots.

Stepper took the bit in his teeth and raced as the darkness settled deep over the land. The horse got his second wind and raced on, southward, a dark wraith flying before the wind of his wake, flying like the wind itself, whipped on by fear and the odd feel of the lump on its back. His master wasn't in command. A dead weight rode his shoulders. The horse smelled blood and sweat and fear. Its eyes rolled white in their sockets. His nostrils flared with exertion and strain.

Mile after mile, Stepper raced, then slowed.

The air changed.

The scene of water and grasses and cattle musked the air, weighted it with poignant aromas. A screech owl trilled. Bats sliced through the air, fangs bloodied from the rising sea of insects. A cow bawled.

Lights flickered just ahead.

But Blood didn't see them. He didn't hear the challenge hurled into the night.

His left arm cradled the saddle horn in a death grip.

When the horse stopped, he slid from the saddle. His body drummed heavily on the ground.

Voices swelled up about him.

A hand-held lantern swayed in the darkness, bathing him in a wobbly circle of light.

It lit the blood that drenched his hips and legs; lit the pale bone of his face so that it resembled a skull, a hideous death-mask, waxen in the wavering glow of the lantern.

"It's Jack Blood," said Luke Cordwainer. "And he's stone dead. Or damned near it."

A woman screamed.

Stepper whickered quietly, casting a gimlet eye on his fallen master.

Chapter Ten

Monte Jubal snapped the frayed matchstick in half with his teeth. "Harry, you ain't got the sense God gave a coon! You peckerwood! I didn't tell you to set fire to Blood's place."

"Hell, I thought you'd be mighty proud we burned him out."

"Yair? Well, where in hell's Deke?"

"I told you. I don't know." Mapes sat at the back table in the Lone Wolf, wondering when Jubal was going to offer him a drink of whisky. The bottle sat between them. The barkeep had brought the extra glass over at least five minutes ago. It was mid-morning and Mapes had ridden all night from Dragoon. Breakfast had been put away three hours before. It had taken him a good two hours to find Jubal. He had looked for him at the Occidental and at the Orient, but here he was holed up in a second-rate saloon with rooms in back and upstairs.

"Don't know, or don't want to know?" Jubal sneered.

"Hell, he might have made it. I just saw his horse, that's all. And his horse didn't make it."

"Deke was a pretty good man."

Jubal spat out splinters of wood, searched through

his vest for a fresh matchstick. He was still bleary-eyed from a night out on the town. Tombstone was wide open, split into factions of hardcases. As long as a man kept to his own bunch, he was all right. It was when he tried to get in good with one or another of the other bunches that he was liable to be back-shot. Curly Bill Brocius and his men were holding their own with Wyatt Earp and his faction. But the tension in town was like a wet strip of rawhide drying in the sun. Ever since the Clantons and the Earps and Doc Holliday had shot it out at the O.K. Corral, nobody trusted anybody else in Tombstone.

"Deke was right enough," ventured Mapes, licking his dry lips.

"That's all? What about Blood. You see him after that?"

"He's likely dead, Jubal. You gonna share that whisky?"

Jubal snapped his head back as if cuffed by a bear.

"What?" he roared. "Blood dead?"

"Maybe. I shot him. Shot him bad."

Jubal's eyes narrowed to feral slits.

"You sonofabitch," he breathed. "He was mine. Mine!"

"Dammit, Jubal, just listen, will you? The man was pressing me hard. He probably blowed Deke out of the saddle and then come after me. I was just defending myself. Got him good, too." A flicker of a smile played on the corners of Harry's mouth.

"You better tell me all of it, Harry."

Jubal shoved the bottle angrily across the table. Mapes picked it up on the fly and ran a healthy stream of whisky down the spout and into his glass. He took the bite and his eyes watered. He held on until the nausea settled and the warmth spread through his gut. The barkeep at the rough board bar eyed him as he trimmed the bottles on the back bar.

"Ah," breathed Harry, with a shudder of pleasure. "That takes the kinks out of the backbone. I been ridin' hard all night."

"Get to Blood."

"The man's a tracker. Horse all tuckered out and he stuck to me like furniture glue. So, I figured I'd circle him and get the drop on him. He'd have the sun square in his eyes and then it would be dark in case I didn't make it. I had him cold, Jubal. First shot hit him in the leg. Any other man would have howled and gone flying out of the saddle. Blood stuck. I blasted him fast as I could shoot, hit him again. I don't know, the back, the lung."

"And so he dropped?"

Harry shook his head, toyed with his glass.

"Hell, he took off. That big horse of his fair went flying. It was dark as the inside of a coal mine by then, but I took off after him. Found his hat. Blood all over it. Blood trail for a long ways."

"So where is he?"

"Dead, I reckon, I backtracked, saw all the blood. Like a gut-shot deer. Hell, he wouldn't have made five miles. I figger he's bein' picked over by turkey buzzards right about now."

Jubal looked unconvinced. He stroked his beard, chewed on the matchstick.

"You sure that's what happened, Harry? I don't want no surprises. I got things set up here now and I'd hate like hell for them to get spoiled."

"I swear," said Harry. He tossed back the last of his drink, wiped his damp lips with his sleeve.

Jubal poured him another drink. Drank a finger

of his own. He was pacing himself, but now he felt he could relax. A man hit that bad wouldn't come walking in unexpected. Blood was either dead or so bad wounded he would be stove up for a long time. Or, he might die sometime soon. Jubal cracked a forgiving smile.

"Hell, you did good, Harry. Saved me the trouble. I just wisht you'd brought me back a piece of his black hide, that's all."

"I got his hat out in my saddle bags. Bloody as a monthly rag."

Jubal grinned. He motioned to Pancho, who had finished the bar and was sneaking a bean-filled tortilla into his mouth. He slipped the morsel back under the counter and shuffled over to the table.

"The one was here, yesterday," Jubal said. "Curly. Fetch him. Not Brocius, but the *pelón*. You savvy?"

"*Sí*. Curlee. He aslip now. No hair. *Pelado*. I get him for you, *Señor* Jewball."

"Curly?" asked Harry. "Curly Bill?"

"No, this is another Curly. This one don't have hair like Bill Brocius. He's pure bald. Bald as a cue ball."

Harry screwed up his face. Shook his head.

"Don't know him."

"He might work out. Now that Deke's gone and Cooper's under cover, we need another man." Quickly, Jubal briefed Mapes on what Cooper had done. He didn't tell him that Curly Adams was no more than a footpad who would sell out his employer, if not his best friend. He wasn't in the habit of telling his confederates all that he did and in this case, he was not proud. It was just as bad to pay a man for betraying a friend as it was to betray one. Yet he had no conscience about what he had done. Blood got what he deserved. In fact, he had lived too long with a woman that hadn't belonged to him.

Jubal had another drink of the good whisky. Mapes filled his own glass without asking.

Curly Adams appeared, disheveled, carrying his boots in his hand. He sat down, slipped them on while Pancho went back to his clandestine tortilla.

"Curly, this here's Harry Mapes. Shake hands, boys, and then let's take a walk. Walls have ears."

"What's up?" asked Curly.

"We'll see," said Jubal, lurching to his feet. He wasn't drunk. He had an enormous capacity for alcohol. It was a thing he had once been proud to boast, but now he wondered if it wasn't a curse. It took more and more to put him away and he felt worse for a longer time afterward. But good whisky was hard to come by and he couldn't pass up Old Overholt after months of tanglefoot or Taos Lightning.

"Put the bottle back, Pancho. Be back later," Jubal called to the Mexican barkeep.

The bright sun painted the false fronts yellowish-green, the dust-clogged streets a pale lemon. Thin clouds hazed the light, softened the adobes. Jubal turned up Fourth Street, away from the clatter of merchants. A skeletal cur, its shaggy tail curled under its hindquarters, dodged the trio as they took to the center of the street.

"Curly," Jubal said. "You still want to join my outfit?"

"I sure as heck do, Jubal."

"You got to follow orders. No questions."

"I'm your man. I been thinkin' about this a long time."

Mapes said nothing.

Jubal stopped at the corner, looked around. He

tossed away the soaked and shredded matchstick in
his mouth. He looked at the two men.

"Mapes here thinks he put Blood down. He 'dobe-
walled him up in the Dragoons and it might be that
we won't be troubled any more. Still, I took out
some insurance. Yesterday. Now I got to add to it.
Now I can't use Mapes here. Somebody might remember him and me being together. So, it falls on
you, Curly. That man in the sheriff's office, working under Behan, you met yesterday, is one part of
the insurance policy."

Mapes's eyebrows went up.

"Ed Collins," Jubal said.

Mapes nodded. He knew Jubal meant Emmett
Cooper. Collins was an alias Emmett had used from
time to time when dodging the law.

"And the second part?" asked Adams, sliding his
hat off his head and running fingers over his smooth
pate.

Mapes's jaw dropped when he saw the gleaming
head.

"Watch you don't get sunburnt," he cracked wryly.

"He's heard it all before, Harry. Listen." Jubal
pierced Mapes with a look. "Curly, I want you to
report to that deputy and tell him you heard Blood
say he was going to kill his wife and kid and set
fire to his place."

"That's all?" asked Curly.

"That's all. Be right sure about it, too. You heard
him tell you that when you left Fort Huachuca."

"Why?" asked Curly.

" 'Cause Sheriff Behan will take that real serious
if you do a good job of acting and he'll send someone
up to check on it."

Curly whistled in admiration.

Mapes, too, looked at Jubal with a new respect.

"Then if Blood shows up in Tombstone, he'll get run into the hoosegow faster'n you can say Peckerwood Holler," said Mapes. "I got to hand it to you, Monte Jubal, you don't leave no rope ends dangling."

Jubal cracked a smile.

A pair of women in long dresses passed by, their faces shaded by sunbonnets. They carried woven baskets filled with cloth goods purchased on Allen Street from a cut-rate drummer. The men were silent until they passed. But it was time to move on. Too many people were noticing their small huddle at the corner.

The three men turned the corner on Allen, crossed the wide street that even now was lined with horses, mules, wagons. A hurdy-gurdy wheezed mournfully down the street. Snatches of laughter floated from inside one of the bawdier cantinas. This was a street of life, tucked back out of sight, gawdy, raucous, untamed. Saloons and whorehouses dominated the trade. This was where the cheaper rooming houses catered to men on their way up or on their way down.

Hal Nevers stared at the trio as they crossed the street.

Their backs were to him as he sat in the shade on the porch of the New Mexico: Rooms 50c and Up.

He recognized Curly Adams. The big bearded man—he had seen him before . . . in the Lone Wolf. He knew his name, too. Monte Jubal. The other man he did not know. But now he knew why Curly didn't want him around any more. If he was hooking up with Jubal, he was getting his wish: to ride with the wild bunch. Any wild bunch. Brocius and Ringo had turned him down. The Earps wouldn't give him the time of day. But there he was with

Jubal and he looked as if he was one of the bunch already.

Hal made note of what he saw. Information was information. It might not mean much now, but it might sometime in the future.

The men passed out of earshot, and Hal dug in his vest for makings. He rolled a fat quirly, found a match, lit it. The smoke bit into his throat, clawed his lungs. He leaned the chair back against the wall of the decrepit hotel. Maybe he wouldn't look for work just yet. He would give it another day or two. See what happened.

Jubal stopped outside a Mexican cantina. It was noisy inside. None of the Mexicans paid any attention to them. That suited Jubal just fine.

"I got a job lined up for us," Jubal said, his voice just barely above a whisper. "Listen close."

Curly and Harry crowded close to Jubal.

A guitar struck up a plaintive series of chords. Someone in the cantina began singing a sad *son huasteco,* full of tears and heartache, a song of love and betrayal and death. Jubal ignored it and raised his voice slightly.

"It's pretty quiet right now," he said. "There's bad blood between Brocius and the Earps. Wyatt got himself appointed marshal and he's off chasing Curly Bill somewhere down around Bisbee or over to Nogales. There hasn't been a stage robbery in weeks."

"So?" asked Curly Adams. "You gonna rob a stage?"

Mapes grinned.

"You don't know how we work, do you, Baldy?"

Curly shook his head.

"Jubal mocks what these other jaspers do. He's a reg'lar damned mockin'bird that's what!"

"Shut up, Harry," Jubal said.

"Hell, Jubal, he's one of us, ain't he?"

"You tell him all this bullshit later. Now we got business."

Jubal outlined the plan quickly. It was simple. Curly's eyes brightened like brass buttons.

"We hit the stage in ten days just outside of Pantano. You get yourself a wig, Curly, and the biggest bandanna you can find. Get a real hairy, curly one. You're gonna be Curly Bill Brocius. We'll have Wyatt Earp in fits. Harry and I'll pack the Greeners, you just be sure you throw down on the shotgunner until we brace them. We won't talk during the robbery, so you got to get it straight before we jerk that stage to a halt."

"You mean we're—I'm supposed to be Curly Bill?" asked Adams.

"You do hear good, don't you?" Jubal asked.

Mapes dug an elbow in Curly's side.

Winked.

"What'd I tell you? Everybody'll be blaming Curly Bill for this one. Earp's looking for him down south, and we make him think the hairy bastard is up north. It's perfect. Jubal, you got a set of brains."

"Fuck you, Mapes," said Jubal. But he was pleased. He had himself a new bunch. It was time to ride.

Chapter Eleven

The voices drifted in and out of his mind like bubbles from a child's pipe. The words were all watery and fluid, almost formless. He couldn't make any sense of them. At times they sounded logical, and at others, they might as well have been in a foreign language. He heard his name every so often and wondered if he was dead. He didn't know if he was awake or not, but thought he might be deep asleep. He couldn't see anything and didn't want to see anything. He thought that if he opened his eyes he would just see a red haze or pitch darkness.

Where was he?

Something cool touched his forehead. Cool and damp.

A voice murmured something soft in his ear.

From far off he felt the heat. A heat that turned to pain when he thought about it. Everytime he thought he would open his eyes and get up, he felt himself sinking back down. Down into a place where there was no air and no words and no sound. A place of quiet pain that was not his pain—just pain ... existing ... next to him. It was close enough to touch if he were capable of touching. He seemed to be floating on the pain at times. At others, he was sure he must be bathing in it. But now, it was just there, somewhere out of reach, throbbing, pulsing, waiting.

The sounds drifted away and he heard only a blood red silence.

The pain rose up to him then, drenching him, sucking away his breath. He felt his mouth opening. He heard himself scream, but there was no sensation of screaming. The sound, like the pain, was his, but somehow disconnected—as if he had two bodies; as if he was one of a set of twins.

The voices came back, like the sounds of animals . . . or birds—chattering, humming, growling.

His ears buzzed and rang.

"Jack! Jack!"

His name! That was his name.

"Ginny!" he screamed.

"Oh, my goodness. He's still delirious. Celeste, bring the soup!"

"Yes, Mother."

Blood's eyes opened feebly. The room swam around him. Pain sawed at his brain. Sawed through bone. A streak of fire raced up his leg. A chunk of molten metal burned into his hip.

"Jesus," he muttered.

"Luke! Come quick!" yelled Roxanne Cordwainer, leaning over the bed.

Blood saw a comely woman in her late thirties, hair bundled up on her head, streaked with gray, soft blue eyes, a strong chin and straight nose that hooked slightly at the end. She wore a pinafore over a simple cotton dress. He felt a hand on his arm.

"Jack," she whispered, "thank God you're awake. Luke will be here in a moment."

"Roxanne?"

"Yes. You're alive! Celeste is bringing some broth. Oh, you impossible man, you! You scared us half to death." She squeezed his arm. He was surprised that he could feel it. And the pain. He tried to turn his head, but the pain brought him up short. He felt the bandages tight around his chest . . . bandages on his back and hips. The room smelled of carbolic acid and liniment and perfume. It had the scrubbed smell of fresh milk on Sunday mornings.

"How'd I get here?" he asked, his mouth full of cotton. His hearing was still off. Roxanne sounded as if she was talking underwater. The ringing in his ears was loud, as if someone had struck a churchbell with a sledge. The single note was steady.

"Don't try to talk. Just listen. Oh, wait a minute, here's Luke."

A tall, slender man with a moustache and side-burns loomed over the edge of the bed. His thin brown hair was slicked back. His shoulders were wide. He stretched out a hand that was small, brown as a gnarled oak knot and just as hard. Blood managed to raise a hand to take Luke's. He felt the squeeze and was again surprised that he had normal feeling.

"Jack, son, you're in a bad way. But we're fixing you up. I sent Antonio up to your place to fetch Ginny and Tío Carlos. Celeste can watch little Jesse while your woman nurses you back to health."

"See, Jack," said Roxanne brightly, "there's not a thing to worry about. Antonio will be here tonight or in the morning with Ginny, little Jesse, and Tío Carlos."

"No," Blood croaked. Pain thundered through his body. He closed his eyes. Closed them like doubled-up fists. "No! Dammit, no!"

Roxanne shrank away from the bed. Luke scowled.

"Now listen, son," he said. "We're only trying to do what's best. You've been out cold for two days and Antonio couldn't go until this morning. Hell, it's taken everyone here a whole lot of time just to keep you breathing. You must've lost ten gallons of blood and I had to cut out a piece of bullet big as your little fingernail that was workin' its way to a mighty big vessel in your leg. There ain't a saw-bones within twenty mile of here."

Celeste entered the room at that moment.

She was a petite young woman of eighteen, with her mother's pale blue eyes, her father's dark hair. Her pert, upturned nose gave her the look of a pixie and when she smiled, deep dimples etched themselves into the corners of her mouth. She was firm-breasted, trim, with a supple, hour-glass figure that refused to stay concealed under the crinoline frock she wore. She carried a tray laden with a steaming cup of broth, a large wooden spoon, and a cast iron pot with the lid on it.

Luke stepped aside to let his daughter pass. Roxanne drifted to the foot of the bed.

"Hello, Jack," Celeste said. "It's good to see you awake. Have some broth." She set the tray down on the table next to the bed and picked up the cup. Blood stared at her, dazed.

"I know you can't sit up," Celeste told him, "so I'll have to hold your head up like I been doin' these past two days. I won't have to feed you with the spoon. You can drink from the cup."

"Huh?" said Blood. "I've been here two days?"

"Three is more like it," said Luke. "And a night. A hellish night."

"You talk, Pa. Jack, you hush and let me feed you this hot broth. You need your strength."

Helplessly, Blood lay there as Celeste expertly

slung an arm around his neck and forced his head up. She put the cup up to his lips, tilted it. Beef, chunks of potatoes, leeks, hot broth, poured into his mouth, down his throat.

Blood allowed Celeste to feed him the broth. He could almost feel its strength flooding him. His hunger was acute and he chewed the beef greedily.

"Good!" exclaimed Celeste, with relief. "We were really worried about you."

Blood lay back, sated. He had put away two mugs of broth.

"Luke," he said weakly, "let me talk to you alone."

Luke looked at his wife and daughter.

"Of course," said Roxanne. "Come on, Celeste, we've things to do."

"Thanks," said Blood. "Both of you. I'm deeply grateful."

"It's our pleasure," said Roxanne. "You'll feel better when Ginny gets here to take care of you."

Blood winced.

Luke waited until the door closed, then drew up a chair and sat by the bed. His weather-tanned face was heavily veined. He had spent most of his life outdoors and the wind and sun had etched hard lines next to his nose, around his mouth, in his forehead. He looked at Blood with concern, the crows feet next to his eyes crinkling into deep furrows.

"What's on your mind, Jack?"

"Antonio's not going to find Ginny, Luke. Or Jesse. Or Tío Carlos. Only their graves. They're all dead."

"Dead? Are you still out of your head, son?"

Blood grimaced.

Haltingly, he told Cordwainer what had happened. He left out nothing except his own shock and grief. He told him of Eli Jubal and Monte, of the burning of the house, the tracking of the two men, Larson and Mapes.

"Mapes suckered me good. I walked right into it."

Luke Cordwainer drew a breath. He shook his head sadly; put a hand on Blood's, squeezed it manfully.

"I'm damned sorry, Jack," he said quietly.

"I'd be obliged if you'd tell the women folk."

"Yeah."

"How bad am I bunged up, Luke?"

"Could be worse. You lost a lot of blood. I took that chunk of lead out, but it was only a splinter. Nothing cut that won't heal. You just gotta take it slow and easy for a time."

"I'm going after Jubal, Luke. And Mapes. Cooper, too. I've got a special boil for that bastard. He's the one that roped Jesse, dragged him."

"Jesus, Jack. You ain't going nowheres for a time. Matter of fact, me and Roxanne were fixin' to go to Tucson when you came in all bloodied up. We got business there that just won't wait. Be gone a week or two, but you can stay here. Celeste can take care of you."

Blood tried to rise. A sickening pain wrenched him back in place.

"Don't try it, Jack," Cordwainer warned. "You lost about a gallon of red juice and it's going to take a lot of beef to get you back on your feet."

Blood nodded.

His eyes were heavy. It was no use trying to do something he couldn't. Luke was right. He needed to build himself back up. Jubal and the others could wait. If they weren't in Tombstone, they'd be somewhere else. He would find them. Even if he had to ride to the ends of the earth. He'd find the bastards!

"When you leaving, Luke?"

"We were going to wait until ... that is, until 'Tonio got back. But we ought to leave right away. Today. It's real important."

"You go on. I'll be okay. Week or two will see me through this. I guess nothing broke."

Luke shook his head.

"You got two clean holes in you. Celeste knows how to pack 'em, change the bandages. She'll be your nurse. She did it all anyway. She does the same for a horse, any of the beeves. Reg'lar little doctorer, she is."

"I owe you much, Luke. You go on to Tucson. Reckon I'll be here when you get back. My horse. . ."

"Stepper's fine. Celeste took him under her wing too. Runs him with the whip purt near ever' day and spoilin' him with grain. He brought you here and I reckon we're mighty grateful for that."

Blood closed his eyes.

Pain washed over him. But already he felt stronger. He was alive. He would heal.

"You get some sleep, son," Luke said. "If I don't see you before we leave, *adiós*."

"*Vaya* . . ." Blood breathed. His eyes fluttered. He sank back down into somnolence, let the broth do its work. He was asleep before Luke closed the door.

*   *   *

He awoke in darkness. His mouth was dry. A rumbling pain throbbed in his hip, answered by a throb in his lower back. His tongue flicked over dessicated lips.

"Water!" he whispered to himself.

His eyes adjusted to the gloom. A crack of light seeped under the door. He reached for the glass at his bedside. The pain scorched him from thigh to brain. His fingers closed around the glass.

It fell just as the door opened. The glass hit the floor with a splintering crash as light flooded the room.

Celeste, in a nightgown, stood in the doorway, a lamp in her hand.

"Jack!"

The light bobbled toward him as he sank back on the bed.

"Water!" he said again. "I'm bone dry, Celeste."

She set the lamp on the bedside table. Her slippers crunched on the broken glass.

"Oh, dear. I'll bring you another glass."

"The pitcher. Just give me the pitcher."

She held the pitcher to his lips. Water slopped into his throat. He choked, cleared his air passage and drew the water into his mouth in hungry gulps. Celeste kept pouring. Blood kept drinking. His mouth and throat were parched. The water soothed the arid membranes, softened the parchment-hard tissues. He drank the whole pitcher, lay back exhausted.

She placed a hand on his forehead.

"You've got the fever again."

Blood began to shake with chill.

"I—I'm freezing," he said.

"The water does that, I guess." She stood up, pulled another comforter up over him. Blood continued to shiver. His teeth chattered like dice in a box.

"Celeste," he said. "I think one of my wounds broke open. I feel wet."

"Did you use the bedpan?" she chided.

"Jesus, Celeste."

"Don't swear." She smiled at him warmly. "I'll

have to turn you over. It's probably that back wound.
The one Pa took a sliver of lead out of. He had to cut
it some. I sewed you up, but you might have slipped
a stitch."

"You sewed me up?"

"Just like a rag doll."

He looked at her helplessly. The woman had
worked on him and he didn't know anything about
it. It was just as well. He had no clothes on. She
would have had to see him that way. It was probably she who emptied the slop bucket too—what she
called a bedpan. It was pure hell trying to use the
damned thing. All that soup.

Celeste gently turned him over on his stomach.
She did it so deftly, he thought she must have
trained to be a nurse, but he knew that wasn't so.
She was just like a hundred other women in the
territory. They learned how to make do with what
they had. What they had was a lot of uncommon
common sense.

He felt the bandage come off. A slight tearing
sound, pressure on his flesh.

"You've got a little ooze. Infected, probably. That's
why you have the fever."

"Dammit, I'm cold!"

"Hush now, swear-mouth. I'm going to put some
healing herbs on there and then I'll see to it that
you're warm."

"Hell, I'm smothering under blankets."

"There are other ways to keep warm," she said
softly.

Chapter Twelve

Blood's fever raged, off and on, for a week. Celeste hovered over him constantly, like a ministering angel. He was only dimly aware of her. Once, he thought he had touched a bare breast. Another time, he felt a bare leg against his. It was difficult to separate dream from reality.

Once, Antonio came in to see him, weeping and wringing his battered hat in his hands. He spoke wildly in Spanish, expressing sympathies over Blood's wife and son, bewailing the fact that Tío Carlos—beloved Tío Carlos Avila—had been killed and his daughter on her way here from Sonora. Poor Avril Avila, orphaned now, out of the convent and expecting to embrace her father. What would she do now? All alone and her only relative buried under a heap of stones in the devil's own country? Celeste had shooed Antonio away, protecting Blood from visitors.

She moved in and out of his room like an angel so that he wondered, at times, if he was alive or dead and possibly in heaven.

He knew that she had kept him warm with her own body heat. It was something he did not want to talk about just yet. It staggered him that she could

105

do that for him. When he was awake, he was em-
barrassed to know this thing. He avoided looking at
her directly, but only gazed at her when she was
busy doing something else and did not look him in
the eye.

When the fever broke, he knew he was finally on
the mend.

Celeste came in with a breakfast tray. Blood sat
up. There was no pain, only a couple of tugs where
the wounds were.

"My, but you look human this morning," she said
gaily. "Or you will after I shave you."

He felt his face. A thick growth of beard scratched
his fingers.

"Ouch," he laughed.

She set the tray on his lap, touched his forehead.
He looked her in the eyes. Close. There was something there. A light. Compassion. Tenderness. His
heart sank. Celeste was beautiful. He wondered if
he had fallen in love with her so soon after losing
Ginny. No, it was just a curiosity. He had heard
stories from men who had fought in the war, about
falling in love with their nurses. Some of the nurses
were hags, but that didn't make any difference.

Celeste returned his gaze, strong for a moment,
full of meaning. Then, she dropped her eyes shyly.

"Thank you, Celeste," he said. "I'm mighty glad
you pulled me through."

"Oh, pshaw, you're strong. I noticed you didn't
use the bedpan last night."

"I got up, went outside."

"Did it hurt?"

"Not much. My muscles are all kinked up, though."

"You'll be sore and tender for a while. Now, eat
your breakfast while I boil some water. I'm going to
shave you, whether you like it or not. You scratch."

They both blushed.

Blood looked down at the tray. There were eggs, biscuits, bacon, beans, a thin strip of beefsteak, a steaming cup of black coffee. He attacked the breakfast voraciously as Celeste tripped out of the room. He felt a tug at his loins when he saw her rounded behind bouncing under a pale cotton dress. He was ashamed of himself for even looking, for thinking what he had thought for the briefest moment.

The solid food was the first he'd had in ten days. He drank three cups of coffee before Celeste accused him of stalling so that he wouldn't have to get a shave.

"Not true," he said. "But I can shave myself."

"You can, but I'm used to it. You have a nice soft face."

"You chide me, Celeste."

"Well, you've been a pretty sick boy. No need to look like a grizzly bear, is there? I enjoyed shaving you."

"I can't thank you enough."

She brought the hot water, lathering soap, a brush, mug, and straight razor. Blood admired her dexterity. The truth was, he didn't know if he could have managed to shave himself. Lying down, maybe, but his legs were still weak. He enjoyed the touch of Celeste's hands. Ginny wouldn't mind, he knew. Or would she?

He had to stop thinking that way. Ginny was gone. Somehow, he was alive. There were men he had to see. That was the only reason for his existence now. Later, perhaps, he could piece together what had happened, come to some agreement with himself. Ginny was still strong in his memory, but he couldn't let her weigh him down. Celeste was a good woman, no more than a girl, really, and she had become mighty important. If it wasn't for her taking care of him, he probably wouldn't have made it.

"When're your folks coming back?" he asked, as she was rubbing his face clean of lather.

"Antonio brought a letter from them yesterday. Came to Benson. They'll be back soon."

"Soon?"

"A few days. A week. I wish they'd take another month, don't you?"

He looked into her cobalt eyes, trying to fathom if there was any meaning beyond her words. Her smoky depths told him nothing, but there was the faintest curl to her lips as if she was cautioned not to reveal a hidden secret.

"It's a long time," he faltered. "A month."

"You need a month of peace and quiet."

She was right, he knew. It would be at least a month before he could sit his saddle without tearing something loose. Still, a month with Celeste could be like a year in an Apache war camp. She was a young, desirable woman, and he was a widower. It was like mixing fire and gasoline. He vowed to give her no reason to test his will power, his resolve to keep to his own side of the fence. He hoped Luke and Roxanne would be back soon.

"I'd like to take a bath sometime this morning," he said, "and get some clothes on. Maybe I could sit outside in the sun this afternoon."

"I gave you a bath every day, Mister Blood."

"You did?" His jaw dropped a good inch.

"Such as it was."

"You have me at the corner post," he said. "I didn't know."

"Well, there's a lot of you to wet and lather, Jack."

He changed the subject as he felt the heat rise up his neck, tingle his face.

"What's Luke doin' down in Tucson, anyways?"

"He sold three hundred horses and he wants to invest some of the money. He was to meet a man in Tucson."

Blood whistled.

"Luke's got a head on his shoulders. He's done right well. Not like me and my three-up outfit."

"Don't talk that way, Jack. Pa said you did just fine after starting out with not enough beef to hold a barbecue. He and Ma started out worse'n you did and it took them longer to get out of the well hole."

"Breakin' horses is a lot harder than growin' beeves."

"Except in this country, where grass is scarcer'n hen's teeth."

Blood laughed. Celeste had a head on her shoulders. She could give tit for tat. He threw up his arms in mock surrender.

"What's this about Tío Carlos's daughter Antonio was babbling about? Did I dream that?"

"No, it's true, I'm afraid." Celeste cleared away the shaving paraphernalia, stacking it with the dishes on the tray. She brushed crumbs from his bed, pushed back a stray hair dangling next to her ear. "Avril Avila is due to arrive in Nogales day after tomorrow. Antonio's going to fetch her. I imagine we'll take her in, if she wants to stay."

"Tío set great store by her. Talked of that girl a heap."

"He thought a lot of you, too, Jack. And he loved little Jesse."

"I know. I miss them terrible, Celeste. I guess I always will."

"I'm sorry. I shouldn't have—"

"No. I can't keep burying it. It happened. You can't pussyfoot around me. It would make me damned nervous."

Celeste swooped up the tray and started for the door.

"You know, Jack," she said, "you curse too damned much!"

They both laughed, and Blood was still chuckling after she had gone. The pain seemed to go away when she was around.

It was a bad sign.

Or a good one.

* * *

Jack lay on the bed, hands folded behind his head, his arms winged on the pillow. He listened to the night sounds—crickets tuning up like a scattered orchestra of sawyers, a coyote yapping on a ridge, a horse nickering for reassurance in the corral.

The guest room, where he was staying, was sparsely furnished, but Celeste had spruced it up with bright flowers Antonio had given her. He had not noticed the room at all until the past couple of days. A religious picture hung on one wall, a Currier & Ives in a cheap frame on another. Deep windows with outside shutters were sunk into the adobe, a gun port was cut in the wood. A bedside table, a highboy dresser, another table and a pair of high-backed chairs streaked with the remnants of the original varnish, and a wardrobe in one corner, where his patched clothes and pistol hung, completed the furnishings. He would have to buy clothes and a new rifle.

The wounds were healing fast. Herbs and the salt baths had crimped the stitched flesh, closed off the leaks. The wounds itched now and had changed color. Good signs. The infection was gone. Sun and good food had furthered the healing process. Exercise—careful exercise—had strengthened the melding flesh underneath the stitches. There was little pain, just a twinge now and then, a tug at a sore spot if he moved too fast or tried to bend over. He was putting on weight, but that was all right. He had lost some pounds during the fever time.

Celeste had been good to him—good for him— never crowding him, letting him go at his own pace, like a babe trying to learn how to walk. She never mentioned the nights she had lain with him, heating his body with hers as he rattled with chill. Nor had he said anything. But it was between them. And, sometimes, when he looked at her from a distance, he thought she was Ginny. Hoped that it had all been a dream and Ginny was alive, bustling about the house, fixing his meals, preparing his bed.

He could not sleep now, thinking of her. Not Ginny. Celeste.

It had gotten worse after Antonio had left that morning. Knowing they were alone together. All alone. The tension had been there, although neither had acknowledged it. His loins swarmed with heat now, thinking of her. Thinking of those brief glimpses of her naked beside him in bed. Of her warm touches, between deliriums.

A chorus of coyotes began yapping, bright ribbons of animal laughter floating on the clear night air. Maybe they were chasing deer or rabbits. Playing. A female in heat, perhaps. Stepper whinnied. He was like a man whistling in the dark, hoping nothing would happen, but secretly sure that something would happen. In the dark, each shadow was a danger, a threat. In the dark, a man's thoughts were sometimes crazy.

He wished the lamp were lit. He wished he were a hundred miles away—away from temptation.

Moonlight limned the window sill, seeped into the room, shrouding it with pewter dust.

The house stirred with movement.

Lamp glow wavered down the hall, came toward him. He pulled the sheet over his nakedness. Just a sheet? What the hell was he trying to do? You could see through the damned thing, for Chrissakes!

"Jack? You awake?"

"Huh? Yeah, I guess so."

"Me, too. I can't sleep." She floated into the room, a pale nightgown clinging to her naked body. The cloth rustled against her bare legs. Her face glowed copper-orange behind the lamp's glass chimney. Her features were softened by the shadows, her eyes brilliant glitters, sparkling with light.

"It's so quiet. The horses are jumpy." She set the lamp next to the bed, sat on the edge.

She was close. Close enough to touch. Spirals of soft hair coiled down from her temples, framed her delicate face. He smelled her musk, scarcely hidden by the faint perfume she wore. He propped himself up with an elbow, rolled over on his side, looked at her in the lampglow. Moonlight caught in hair, a silver tangle in the fine wisps. He didn't say anything. He didn't trust himself to say a word just then.

"Antonio will be back tomorrow," she said. "With Avril."

"Yes."

"Pa and Ma could come any time. Not tonight though. Tomorrow. Next day." Her voice was edged with sadness.

"Celeste," he husked, "it's not right, you know. For either of us."

"What?" Her eyes widened in surprise. "Oh! Oh, Jack! Don't. Don't say that. Not now."

"I have to say it."

"No!" She turned, fell on his chest. Her hair tumbled over his shoulders. The sheet slipped down from her weight. She put her arms around him, held him. She was trembling.

"Celeste...."

"Oh, God, I know it's wrong. It's too soon. I'm horrible. But I want you, Jack Blood. More than anything in the world, I want you. Please, don't send me away. I couldn't bear it. I couldn't!"

He slipped an arm around her back. Her sobs shook her body. Tears fell on the tangled hairs of his chest—hot tears that burned his flesh, stirred something deep inside him.

His loins teemed with fire.

His manhood hardened at her nearness.

Her face brushed against his. Her lips grazed his own.

The kiss was like a knife thrust in his groin.

A stab of sweet delicious pain ripped through his spine, set his nerves tingling.

Her tongue slipped between his lips, into his mouth.

"Celeste," he said, breaking the kiss, "are you sure? Damned sure?"

"Yes, oh, yes, Jack. I've wanted you for a long time. Every night. It's been terrible. I hurt all over. Inside."

"I know," he whispered, brushing a hand over her hair. "God, I know."

It was too late to stop now. He couldn't stop. He wanted her too.

Savagely, tenderly, he crushed her in his arms. Drew her against his hardening stalk. He kissed her hard on the mouth, blotting out the guilt, the grief, the last of his resolve.

"Take me, Jack Blood," she moaned, her nipples taut thumbs digging into his chest. "Take me now!"

Quickly, he slipped her gown from her shoulders.

He tossed it to the floor, like something discarded from his past.

She came to him, naked, eager, her lips pursed in anticipation.

He wanted her, then, more than anything in the world.

He wanted her because he was alive again and because she could strip away his past for a while.

He kissed her and the fires in their loins raged out of control.

Chapter Thirteen

Her body writhed, burnished copper by the lamp glow. She swarmed over him, rubbing, burning, caressing. He took a breast in his hand, kneaded its nugget-hard nipple. Felt her shudder as if a charge of electricity had passed through her. Her mouth was wet, warm, tasted of nuts and crushed berries.

"Now!" she whispered, sliding her mouth from his. "Take me now!"

He rolled away to the side, turned her in his arms. She lay on her back, looking up at him, her eyes flickering with lamplight, sparkling with fresh tears. He rose above her, muscles corded, loins poised. She looked at his wavering stalk, gleaming with smeared juices on the flanged crown.

She gasped with pleasure.

He sank into her as her legs spread wide to receive him.

A sudden shudder rippled through her flesh. Her legs twitched upward as if galvanized. Blood slid into the steaming tunnel of her sex, slow. He paused as the leathery barrier of girlhood stopped his stroke.

"Celeste," he said, "you didn't tell me."

"I—I was afraid you-d . . . you'd be mad."

"Mad?"

"Mad or—disappointed."

"I'm not either. But you should have told me."

"Does it make a difference?"

"Not to me. Maybe to you. To your future husband."

She sucked in a breath, looked up at him with wide eyes.

"I don't care," she said. "Do it to me. Break it."

"It doesn't have to break, you know. You can still have pleasure and save it for your man."

She closed her eyes, trying to shut out the tears. They leaked onto her face, ran down her cheeks.

"It wouldn't be the same, though, would it?"

"Not quite. It's a big decision. Your father might want to tack my hide on the barn door."

"He won't know. Please, Jack. I'm a woman. I want to be a woman. I want all of you inside me. I want to remember this first time. Isn't that important, too?"

"Yes."

He stroked her slowly, pushing against her maidenhead.

"Will it hurt much?" she asked.

"I don't know. Maybe a little."

"I could feel you there. A tug."

"Scared, Celeste?"

"Some."

"Best to loosen your cinch straps. Don't tighten up."

"All right," she said, her voice quavering.

Blood took it slow and easy. Gentle strokes. Soft batterings against the rubbery hymen, weakening the membrane with each nudge and thrust. His cock was bone-hard, swollen with engorged blood. It filled the crevice of her sex. Each thrust-stroke brought a sigh of pleasure. Each bump against her maidenhead brought a slight twinge of pain, a fleeting razor sear on the nerve-ends, slight as a mild toothache.

He felt the membrane stretch and weaken. His own juices boiled. His manhood throbbed, the thick veins in the stark blue relief. He rammed her, harder and harder, watching her eyes to see if the pain was too much. Her eyes swam with light, with joy. And his own pain was forgotten, a distant throb at two points or three that he favored slightly by supporting his own weight on his strong hands and wrists.

"I love it, Jack," she breathed. "It's wonderful. It won't hurt. I know it won't. Break it. Break it now!"

Blood stroked faster, deeper. He rammed hard when he felt the resistance from the hymen. Celeste gave a little cry as the leathery barrier separated, tore free. Blood rammed through, buried his shaft clear to the mouth of her womb.

Celeste shrieked and clasped his back with both arms, squeezed him. Her body shuddered with a sudden, shattering orgasm. She squealed with delight as he probed her steaming tunnel again and again with swift searing strokes.

He felt his own seed boil. He grasped her tightly as the explosion rocked him. His senses soared as orgasmic convulsions shook him from head to toe. A sharp twinge of pain shot through the wound in his leg. The convulsions passed. Beneath him, Celeste trembled, her body quivering as waves of pleasure washed over her.

She held him tightly.

Tears gushed from her eyes.

"Sad?" he asked.

"Happy, very happy. Thank you, Jack. You made me a woman."

He rolled off of her, lay on his back. He cast a sidelong glance at her, gazed at her in wonder.

"No," he said, "you were already a woman. Nobody ever noticed before."

* * *

The Overland Stage lumbered out of Pantano, furls of dust streaming in twin spirals behind the boot. Six horses strained at their harness straps as the driver yelled and cracked a thin whip over their heads. The stage was running an hour late and Knut Jensen, the drover, worked his team as if they were mules. The shotgun man, Ben Thomas, hung onto the rail, dug in his boot heels, as the coach swayed, gaining momentum.

Inside the Concord, Luke Cordwainer savored the aroma of a cheroot, carefully blowing the smoke out the window. Roxanne fanned herself with a paper fan bought in Tucson, moving the hot air against her face to give her the sensation of coolness. The other passenger, a drummer from St. Louis, who had ridden all the way from Ramona in California, was a florid-faced man in his late thirties who had spent too much time with John Barleycorn. Spiderwebs—thin red lines—laced his face. His cheeks were purpling, the pores oversized to the point of almost being pocks. He sipped from a bottle of medicant that fooled no one. The fumes from his breath reeked inside the careening coach.

"Well, we're getting closer to home," said Roxanne. "I can't wait to see Celeste's face when I show her all the pretties I bought her."

"I just hope she can handle the situation there," said Luke, expelling a plume of smoke out the window. The smoke was snatched by the wind and swallowed up by the rooster tails of dust spooling out of the Concord's wheeltracks.

"You mean Jack Blood?"

"I do. He's a handful. Taking care of a wounded man can be choresome."

"Are you talking about me, Luke Cordwainer?" Roxanne squeezed his arm teasingly. "The time you were all stove up from being caught afoot by that old mossyhorn. Why, you were a baby, until you started getting better. Then you were ornery. Downright onery."

"I'm talking about that time. And others. Man not used to being bedridden gets mighty touchy at being waited on hand and foot."

"You loved it," she chided.

"For about ten minutes. Jack will want to be up and about and Celeste will try and keep him down. We stayed away too damned long."

"Antonio's there. He'll keep an eye on things. Celeste needs help, Antonio can give it to her."

"Yair. Guess so."

The drummer looked at the two seated across from him. His rheumic eyes tried to focus in the swaying compartment.

"Someone sick at home?" asked Amos Winstead. "Happens I drum a line of medical products that are the finest in the land, bar none. And not just one brand, either. Nor any homemade snakebite remedies. No, sirree, sir, you bet your bottom dollar, Amos Winstead sells only the best. What ails the child?"

"Bullet wounds," growled Luke. "Lead poisoning. You got any cure for that?"

Winstead seemed to shrink in his seat as Cordwainer withered him with a stern look.

"Sorry," said the drummer. "Just trying to help. The

name's Amos Winstead. I hail from Ellsworth, in Kansas Territory. Work out of St. Louis."

Luke blew a plume of smoke straight at Winstead. Roxanne kicked his boot, shot him a disapproving glance.

Winstead hacked, sipped from his bottle of medicant.

"For a cough," he said, pointing to the dark bottle with raised lettering on the glass.

"Likely you'll cure your thirst from the same flask," cracked Luke.

"Luke, why don't you take a nap," said Roxanne. "You're awful tired."

He was tired. He looked out the window, heaved a sigh. The land shimmered with heat. Off to the right, sunlight glinted on something metallic, silver. He blinked his eyes. Looked again. The stage slowed, pulling a grade. The metal was moving, passed out of his line of sight.

He sat up straight, stuck his head out the window. The hill was steeper than he thought. Ahead he saw nothing but huge boulders lining the road. The air smelled of horse sweat and mesquite.

"What is it, Luke?" asked Roxanne.

"Nothing. Probably nothing." He paused. "I don't know."

The horses strained to pull the wagon up the grade. It was slow going, but the dust wasn't so bad inside the coach. The passengers could hear Jensen yelling at the animals, cracking his whip over their heads.

Luke stuck his head out the window again. The summit was not far off. Another three hundred yards. He could no longer see over the top. Boulders lined both sides of the road. It was a bad spot. He had seen something out there. Something that was not quite right. He didn't like it. But, there was no need to worry Roxanne. And the drummer didn't have much of a brain. What he did have was pickled in alcohol.

Luke's hand slid to his sidearm. He loosened the Colt Peacemaker in its holster.

Just in case.

He leaned back out, looked up at the shotgunner. He saw part of his leg, an arm, the sawed-off Greener held loosely in his hand. Ben Thomas didn't appear worried from the way he sat. Luke shrugged.

"What do you keep looking out there for?" asked his wife.

"Just seeing how far we had to go to clear the grade," he lied.

He stubbed out his cigar, stuck the remainder in his shirt pocket. He might have seen quartz glinting in the sun or flakes of mica embedded in the rocks. He doubted either possibility, but there was no use worrying over nothing. He restrained himself from looking outside the coach again. At least he and Roxanne were facing forward. The drummer faced the rear, his rumpled clothes sweat-soaked, rimmed here and there with rosy dust.

The Concord topped the rise and came to a dead stop.

The passengers were pitched from their seats. The drummer toppled onto the floor. Roxanne bounced atop him. Luke shot into the opposite seat, striking his head on the leather cushion backing. Dazed, he reached out for the holding strap.

Voices, abrupt, loud, stern, carried to the inside of the coach.

"You climb down off'n that seat, gunner," said Mapes.

"Keep your hands high, driver," said Curly, wearing a wig under his wide-brimmed Stetson.

"Toss down that strongbox," ordered Monte Jubal. "Be quick, or be dead!"

Luke clamped a hand over Roxanne's mouth as she opened her mouth to scream. He grabbed one arm and helped her to her seat. Amos Winstead grumbled, looked up at a bare thigh where Roxanne's skirt had pulled up over her leg.

"What the hell's going on?" he blurted.

"Shut up!" Luke husked, drawing his six-gun.

Roxanne looked at her husband in stark terror.

"Hold up," whispered Luke. He pulled the side curtains, plunging them into darkness stippled with sunlight. Dust motes twinkled in the still air.

They heard the strongbox crash to the ground.

"Ain't you Curly Brocius?" asked the shotgunner, Thomas.

"Shut up!" snapped Jubal. Then: "Curly, open up that coach."

Luke tensed.

The door opened, creaking on its hinges.

Roxanne drew back in fright. Winstead paled beneath the glow of his cheeks. Luke held his pistol low, snug against his leg.

"Come on outa there," Curly said. "Move!"

Luke nodded to Roxanne.

She climbed out first, unassisted. Curly backed off. Luke went out the other door.

Winstead panicked.

Instead of following Roxanne out, he threw himself out the other door, right behind Cordwainer.

Unnerved, Curly fired a shot into the coach. He fired twice more. Roxanne jerked at each sound. She was in the line of fire.

Jubal rode up on the side where Cordwainer and

Winstead had come out, waving a Winchester. The bluing was gone from the barrel. It reflected dazzling light in the sun. He wore a bandanna over his face.

Winstead stared at Jubal. He crouched, pointed a finger.

"I know you!" he shouted. "Jubal! From Ellsworth—"

Jubal shot him in the throat.

A spray-cloud of blood sparkled in the air as the bullet ripped through the larynx, severing muscle and tissue before exploding the spine into splintered bone fragments. Amos Winstead's scream was choked off. His legs danced crazily as his head flopped to his shoulders, the sightless eyes fixed in a glazed stare.

Luke stood, held his arm straight out and hammered back the Colt .45. He squeezed the trigger.

But Jubal was moving, spurring his horse straight at Cordwainer. The shot missed.

Jubal jacked a fresh shell in the chamber, threw his arm straight out and squeezed the rifle's trigger. It went off with a roar in Luke's face. Orange flame scorched the air. Black powder struck his face. The bullet, on a downward path, struck him in the shoulder, skidded off of bone and tore through ribs, ripped the lung sac in its flight downward. The lead ball lodged in his hip.

Luke twisted away in pain.

"Come on, Curly," Jubal shouted. "Let's ride."

Mapes rode up, leered at Roxanne. Curly grabbed up the strongbox and rode off while the other two men covered him.

Roxanne rushed to her husband's side.

Knut Jensen came down beside her.

"He ban hurt purty bad," he said. 'Ve get him in the coach."

The air exploded as Ben Thomas fired both barrels of the Greener after the fleeing horsemen.

They were out of range.

He swung down from the seat, came to help Knut.

"They got away," he said.

"Help me, Ben, by golly. This man ban hurt purty bad, I t'ink."

"Roxanne," croaked Luke. "I—I'm dying. Tell Jack. It was Monte Jubal."

"Please," she begged. "Don't go, Luke. I need you. Celeste needs you." Her face was pale, her voice trembling with fear.

Luke's eyes closed. He shuddered. His eyes opened again, frosted over with the pale cast of death.

"I'm coming," he whispered to no one.

And he was gone.

Roxanne collapsed over him, sobbing.

That's when Ben and Knut noticed the blood on her back.

Chapter Fourteen

Antonio sighed. His ears hurt. One in particular. His right ear. That's the side Avril Avila had sat on all the way from Nogales in the northbound. A constant stream of talk. Questions. He had answered them all a dozen times. How had her father died? Why wasn't Blood there to help him? What was going to be done about it? Why did he work for gringos? How far was the Cordwainer ranch? Endless. Tiring. Questions, *hijo de mala leche, preguntas y preguntas!*

Avril was petite with raven black hair, nut-brown eyes, pearshaped as a fawn's, spit curls dangling next to her ears, a mantilla of black lace on her head, full lacy dress, high-heeled, lace-up boots. She looked like a grandee's lady. A mole was next to her full lips and she had breasts that pushed against her bodice with the persistence of pouter pigeons strutting a mating dance.

"We will be there soon," he said, stepping from the coach. The stage had pulled up in Benson, where he'd left the spring wagon and the dappled gray. "It is only a very few short little miles."

He helped her down. They were the only two passengers, since the stageline carried mostly freight

125

from the East to the border towns. It was to meet
the Tucson stage then return by way of Tombstone.

"Antonio, do not forget the luggage," commanded
Avril.

"I will not forget." He looked up at the two men
on the buck seat helplessly. One of them crawled
back and grabbed the two valises. One was a large
carpetbag, the other of worn leather. He grunted
from the effort.

"Be careful," Avril said in English. "Do not break
anything."

"Yes, ma'am," said the man sarcastically. "What've
you got in here, gold?"

"My dowry," she said in precise English, her words
only slightly accented. She turned to Antonio and
blistered him in a stream of liquid Spanish. He
dutifully walked over to where the men could hand
down Avril's luggage. He nearly collapsed under
the weight of the leather suitcase. Avril was not
amused. The carpetbag put him on his knees. He
brushed off the dust as he set the bag down.

"I will get the spring wagon," he said. "It's at the
livery."

"Be quick about it. I need a bath. I'm weary. I'm
hungry and thirsty."

"Por seguro," muttered Antonio, lugging the heavy
bags to the porch of the freight office. He puffed
with exertion. He streaked a pair of fingers across
his forehead, pushing back his *sombrero,* and the
stream of sweat flew into the air.

A man came out of the freight office. He was
short, barrel-chested, phlegmatic. His legs were
bowed and he wore an old converted percussion pistol in a worn hide holster. His hat was Montana-
crimped, soiled with the stains of careless living.

"Hold on thar," he said to Antonio, who had started to cross the street.

Avril fanned her face furiously with impatient winglike strokes.

"Yes, *Señor?*"

"You Antonio Martinez?"

The Mexican nodded, his eyebrows raised in quizzical semicircles.

"You get on over to Doc Halliburton's *pronto.*"

"What is the trouble?" asked Antonio.

"Doc and the marshal will tell you all about it, *amigo.* He's the next street over, next to the Grange."

"I know where he is," said Antonio politely.

"I will go with you," said Avril. To the man who had spoken to Antonio, she said; "Please watch my bags while we are gone."

"Yes'm," said the man, turning on his heel and returning to the office.

Avril shot him a dark look, but stepped quickly to catch up with Antonio who was turning into the walkway between the freight office and the barber shop.

There was a crowd in front of Halliburton's, whose modest office was crowded in among a number of false fronts. Wagons lined the street. Men and women milled, chattered, gaped as Antonio and Avril threaded their way through the crowd.

"Was it Curly Bill?" someone asked Ben Thomas.

"Meanest man I ever saw," said Thomas, nodding.

"Knut, did you see who the others were?" asked a man with a butcher's apron swaddling his waist.

"They wore handkerchiefs over their faces, *ja,*" said Jenson.

"Let's get up a posse!" yelled an inebriated young man, with a three-day beard bristling his face.

Antonio went inside, followed by Avril.

A small knot of men stood in the anteroom talking in low tones. One of them wore a badge that proclaimed: U.S. Deputy Marshal. He looked at the pair who had entered, separated from the group of men.

"You Martinez?"

Antonio nodded.

"We got word from Pearblossom's you was due in today. Good thing, too." Pearblossom's was the livery stable. "You work for Luke Cordwainer?"

"Yes."

"He got shot. Dead. The missus is in with the sawbones. Wants to see you. Who's the lady?"

"This is—" Antonio began.

"I'm Avril Consuela Avila y Montez," said Avril, interrupting. "I am on my way to see the Cordwainers."

The marshal looked bewildered. His slate eyes swept Avril up and down, then closed in exasperation.

"I'm Marshal Elvis," he said. "Ken Elvis. You two come with me." He was a mustached, lean man in his forties with pale gray eyes.

The deputy ushered them through the door into the doctor's office. A woman met them and led them to a screen that blocked off part of the room. Roxanne Cordwainer lay on a large bed built against the wall. She was very pale.

Halliburton was bent over her, listening to her heart through a stethoscope. He saw Elvis and shook his head somberly. Roxanne's eyes were closed. Her breathing was very shallow. A white sheet was pulled up to her neck. The doctor removed the stethoscope from under the sheet and stuck the listening end into the pocket of his gray smock.

"You Antonio?" he whispered.

Antonio stared numbly at Mrs. Cordwainer. He took off his hat, worried the brim in both hands. Avril looked at the woman on the bed with sharp glittering eyes.

"She wants to talk to you. I'm Elmer Halliburton. There's not much time. Deputy, take the lady into my office."

Avril shook off his hand as Elvis touched her arm.

"I will stay," she said evenly. The doctor nodded, his brown eyes expressionless. He was a thin rail of a man with a hooked nose, pince nez, graying sideburns. He wore black pin-striped trousers under the smock, polished brown shoes.

Halliburton leaned over Roxanne and whispered something into her ear.

Roxanne's eyelids fluttered, slid back as her eyes opened.

"'Tonio?" she husked. "Is that you?"

"*Si, patrona,* I am here," said Antonio. Elvis nudged him toward the bed.

Roxanne reached out a hand, took his.

"I am sorry, *señora.*"

"Antonio, listen to me." Her voice was a dry cornhusk rustled by the wind. Her forehead was clammy with sweat. The doctor dabbed it with a piece of rolled up gauze. "Luke is gone. He was killed by Monte Jubal. Tell Jack Blood."

The marshal leaned forward, listening intently.

"I will tell him," said Antonio quietly.

"My purse. Take that to Celeste. There is money in it. Tell her I love her."

"I will bring her here," said Antonio defiantly. "I will hurry."

The squeeze on his hand was weak.

Roxanne tried to shake her head, winced.

"No. I—I won't be here tomorrow," she said. "In a little while. . . ."

Tears stung Antonio's eyes, rolled down his cheeks. He squeezed her hand as if to give her some of his strength.

"That's all, son," said Halliburton quietly. "I'll talk to you in my office. Deputy?"

This time Avril did not push his hand away as Elvis took her arm. Antonio's lips quivered as if there was something more he wanted to say. Roxanne shuddered. Her eyes closed. Antonio turned away as he heard her throat rattle with sound. The doctor bent over Roxanne quickly, jerking the sheet away from her bared chest.

A few moments later, he entered his office.

"She's gone," he told Antonio. "I think she just stayed alive long enough to talk to you. Wouldn't say a word to us."

"I'm mighty interested in what she said," said the marshal. "What was that about Jack Blood? You know where he is, Martinez?"

A wary look crept into Antonio's eyes.

"I do not know," he lied.

"Well, we got a flier up from Tombstone today. And a note from Sheriff Behan saying he had murdered his family. I got to look into that. You hold anything back from me and I—"

"Please, Deputy," said Halliburton, removing his pince-nez and wiping them with the tail of his smock. "This is hardly the time or place for an inquisition. Mrs. Cordwainer's dead. You have other duties to perform."

"What happened?" asked Avril. "Was she shot?" Antonio was dumb, staring at the floor. His shoulders sagged under the weight of what he had just experienced.

"Yes," said the doctor. "She sustained severe internal injuries from two gunshot wounds. The woman was brave and strong. I understand her husband succumbed at the scene."

"The stage was robbed," said Elvis. "By three men. One of them, we think, was Curly Bill Brocius. What was that about a Jubal? A Monte Jubal?" He skewered Antonio with a look.

"I don't know who that is," said Antonio honestly. "I must go to the house now and tell her daughter. This is very bad. Very bad. I do not feel so good."

Avril took his arm.

"We will go now," she said. "Thank you, Doctor."

"The remains will be over to the mortuary," said Halliburton. "Miss Cordwainer can come over in the morning to tell Phillips, the undertaker, what she wants done. I'll fill out the death certificates right away."

The marshal nodded to the doctor, walked to the anteroom with Avril and Antonio. The nurse was out there, visiting with the other men.

"You can all go outside now," ordered the marshal. "I got business here. Miss Stevens, you go on back in. The doc needs you."

When the room was cleared, Elvis looked sternly at Antonio. "I'll be out to look around, Martinez," he said. "There's something funny going on and I think you know a lot more'n you're telling."

"No, sir. I don't know nothing."

"Be that as it may, I'm bound to look into this matter. Was Jack Blood in with those holdup men?"

"No!"

"Well, what do you know about his family? He kill 'em, like it says?"

"No. I do not think so."

"Well, you must know something."

Avril stepped up, then, glared at the marshal.

"Marshal, he's told you what you asked. Do not bully this man any more. We will go now." Avril was small, but she stood up on her tiptoes to give authority to her words. The marshal licked his lips as if trying to decide whether to answer her or let them go.

He threw up his hands.

"You," he said to Antonio. "Don't you go anywhere unless you check with me. I may be out there tonight or in the morning. Now go on. I got work to do."

Antonio sighed with relief. Avril took his arm, led him outside.

"Thank you, *Señorita* Avila," he said gratefully. "I am in shock. Poor *Señora* Cordwainer. Poor *Señor* Luke."

"Come on, Antonio," she said, whisking him through the whispering crowd out front. "You are a very poor liar. You whine too much in the face of authority. Now, where is this Jack Blood? My father wrote much about him."

"You will meet him, I think," said Antonio.

"He is at the ranch where we are going?"

"Yes."

"Good. We must help him to escape. Unless he really is a murderer."

"No, he is not a murderer. But he is very sick. He has been shot. I think, by this man Monte Jubal."

Avril swore.

Antonio looked at her in shock. A convent girl, speaking such words. It was not right.

"Oh, come on, 'Tonio," said Avril, "you have heard the words before. Do not be fooled by appearances."

"But the convent . . . the sisters. . . ."

"That was my father's idea. Do you think we girls just sat around and prayed all day? Come on, let's get to the livery before your face freezes and falls off."

Twenty minutes later, the spring wagon bumped and bounced on the road to the Cordwainer ranch. Avril's baggage lay in the back. She pulled her skirt up to her waist.

Antonio almost drove off the road, looking at her legs. They were the finest legs he had ever seen and made him forget his grief for a while.

Chapter Fifteen

Celeste Cordwainer saw the wagon coming from a long way off. A spool of dust funneled into the air. "Someone's coming," she called to Blood. "I think it's Antonio."

Blood hobbled to the door, using a stick as a makeshift cane. He did not want to put much weight on his hips, but he felt stronger than he had in days. He had soaked in a hot tub that morning and sat in the sun for an hour. The new flesh had started to push through the bullet holes, pink and tender. But the seepage was gone, the edges of the wounds toughened up like hide dried in the sun.

"Maybe it's your folks," he said.

"No, that's the spring wagon. They'd be in the surrey."

Blood saw that she was right.

"Antonio must be in a hell of a hurry," he said.

"There you go, swearing again. I declare, Jack, you're a caution!"

They watched as the wagon rumbled up into the yard. Antonio's face was pale under the thin film of dust. Avril sat very stiff on the seat next to him. Antonio sat there, staring at Celeste. Avril punched his arm, said something to him.

"Something's up," said Blood instinctively.

Avril stood up, slapped her dress with flat hands. Dust puffed from the dress. She climbed down and marched to the porch. Antonio sat there, still. He removed his hat, began wringing it in both hands.

"*Señorita* Cordwainer. I am Avril Avila. And you must be Jack Blood. Antonio has swallowed his tongue, so I must be the one to inform you that your parents have been killed. Forgive me for bringing you this bad news. I am so sorry."

Celeste's face fell. Then, a look of disbelief washed over her features. She gasped for breath. The blood drained from her face and her knees buckled. Jack stepped to her side, put an arm around her for support.

Celeste looked at Antonio for confirmation. He nodded solemnly.

"Oh, no!" she shrieked.

Avril rushed up to her.

"I will take her inside," she said to Blood, who looked at Avril dumbfounded as the Mexican girl grasped Celeste's arms and led her inside the house. He stood there for a long moment, frowning.

"Antonio, you'd better explain all this to me before we go in."

Sheepishly, Antonio climbed down from the spring wagon. He pulled the dappled gray over to the hitch rail, slung the reins over it. Stumbling over his words, he blurted out the news of the stage holdup, the shootings, the last moments of Roxanne Cordwainer. Tears flowed copiously from his eyes.

"That's a hell of a note," said Blood.

Antonio looked over his shoulder.

"And this Marshal Elvis will be out here to arrest you very soon, I think."

"He'll play hob," said Blood, his face hardening. "Come on inside."

"No, I will bring in the baggage and unhitch the horse. Do you want me to saddle Stepper?"

Blood considered it. He nodded. He was not ready to ride yet, but it appeared that he had no choice. Jubal had to be stopped and he didn't have time to argue with a U.S. marshal. He turned and went inside the house—to the sound of sobbing.

Both women were weeping. They sat on the overstuffed couch, their arms around each other. Blood hobbled to a chair, stretched out his legs.

"I'm damned sorry, Celeste," he said.

She looked at him with tear-filled eyes.

"Must you always swear? At a time like this, especially! Oh, Jack, what am I going to do?"

He knew she was raving at him out of grief. And somehow he felt responsible. Jubal had dogged his trail for years and now, in a short span of time, he had murdered the people closest to him. It didn't make sense. Was it a quirk of fate or a deliberate plan of diabolical proportions? He let her words wash over him. There had to be some way for the grief, the anger, the hatred to come out. Reason would follow when she found the calm after the storm.

"It's not easy, Celeste," he said quietly. "I'll help all I can."

Avril fixed him with taloned eyes.

"Did Antonio tell you what they are saying?" she asked. "That you murdered your wife, your son, and my father?"

"Yes."

"What?" asked Celeste. "That's not true!"

Avril assessed Blood with her eyes. Looked him up and down.

"Can you ride?" she asked.

"I reckon. If I have to."

"We must go to Benson early in the morning. I would like to go to my father's grave, but that can wait. What will you do, Jack Blood?"

He hadn't quite put a notch in Avril's ear yet. She was a puzzle. She got right to the point. What was he going to do? Celeste needed him. Avril, too, probably. But if he went to town with them, he was liable to walk right into the hoosegow. He was beginning to feel like he'd been ridden hard and put away wet. He was strong enough to travel if he took it easy. He needed another month or so before he would feel topnotch. He didn't have another month, let alone two. Jubal was out there somewhere. Jubal had caused all this grief. The man had bad blood, and now it was affecting them all. He had to be stopped, put down—down deep.

"If you think you can manage, I'll be riding," he told Avril. "To Tombstone."

"That is a good idea. You will hunt the man down who murdered all these people?"

"Yes. I will hunt him down."

Celeste pulled away from Avril's embrace.

"You can't!" she said. "You're not strong enough! Stay here. I—we'll hide you out!"

Blood shook his head.

"I can't stay. I've caused you enough trouble, Celeste. And you, too, Miss Avila."

"My name is Avril," she said. "Did Antonio tell you that the sheriff in Tombstone was looking for you?"

"No, but it figures. Jubal—or a man named Mapes—must have spread the story about me. What can you tell me about the holdup? I reckon it just happened the Cordwainers was on the wrong stage at the wrong time."

"I do not know much. There were three men. One of them was named Curly. And Jubal, of course."

"Curly? Any last name?"

"It was Brocius," said Antonio, puffing in with Avril's valises. He dropped them to the floor with a thud. "Why?"

"Oh, nothing," said Blood. "Curly's getting to be a common name in these parts, that's all."

He'd heard of Curly Bill Brocius, of course—mean as a sidewinder—but he couldn't figure Bill Brocius and Jubal hooking up. Not when Brocius was at odds with the Earps and thick with the Clanton clan. And if Jubal had taken that stage, there should have been four men, including Brocius—Mapes and Cooper, Jubal and Brocius. It was a puzzle. Brocius had his own bunch. And Jubal was every bit the leader Curly Bill was. Two men leading a three-man holdup team? In a pig's squint eye!

"Jack," said Celeste, "I'm sorry I laced into you. You didn't deserve that. You've got your cross to bear, too."

"Don't mention it, Celeste." Blood stood up. "You saddle my horse, Antonio?"

"*Sí.* She is ready. I have tied him in the back." Except for his pronouns, Blood thought, Antonio spoke pretty fair English.

"Good. I'll be obliged if I can get some jerky and hardtack to stick in my saddlebags. I might be a few days, getting to Tombstone the roundabout way."

"Are you going there now?" asked Celeste, the faintest trace of a whine in her voice.

"Soon. But there's something else I have to do first. I think you three can manage without me. I'm sorry I can't go to the funeral, but I better keep

away from the hobbles right now. Celeste, can you
and Antonio do a little lying for me?"

"I don't understand," said Celeste.

"Listen. Both of you. I want you to tell the marshal and anybody else who asks, that I didn't make
it. You say that a bastard name of Harry Mapes
shot me in the back and you buried me next to my
wife and son."

"How can that be?" asked Celeste.

"I'll take care of it. That'll be my first stop. I'll
just put up another grave and tack my name on it
real proper."

"You can't be serious."

"It'll hold Elvis off for a while."

"I should go with you," said Avril. "I want to see
my father's grave."

"No. You stay with Celeste. She'll need you. Give
me a week or so, and I'll be in Tombstone. If you
need me, I'll take a room at the Russ House. Do you
know it?"

The three other people in the room shook their
heads.

"It's on the corner of Fifth and Tough Nut Streets.
If I'm not there, I'll be found at either the Tivoli or
the Capitol Saloon. The Tivoli is on Allen. The
Capitol's at Fourth and Fremont. At Russ House,
I'll register under the name of R. W. Shepp."

"Who's that?" asked Celeste.

"My grandpa on my mother's side."

Blood smiled. He looked at the stick in his hand.
He picked it up and broke it across his knee.

"Here," he said to Antonio, handing him the splintered pieces, "use this for kindling. I won't be needing it any more."

"Before you go," said Celeste, rising, "there's something I want to give you. You'll need it and I know Pa would want you to have it."

She walked over to the fireplace and reached up over the mantle. She took down the new Winchester rifle, handed it to Blood.

He looked at it and at her.

"Thanks," he said. "I'll be mighty proud to own it." He put his arms around Celeste, drew her close. She trembled against him.

Avril's eyes narrowed. She pulled absent-mindedly on a spit curl, took a deep breath.

"Good-bye," Blood said.

He had to tear himself out of Celeste's arms.

Avril was still looking at him with hooded eyes when he left a half-hour later, canteens full, grub in his saddlebags, the new Winchester in his boot.

"I will see you in Tombstone," she whispered to him, out of earshot of Celeste and Antonio.

"You don't have to. . . ."

"I am alone," she said. "I have no family. I will be there. At Russ House."

Something spidery crawled on the back of his neck. She and Celeste were orphans now. Somehow, he felt responsible. But Avril surprised him. She was a tenacious sort. There was weight to her words. A weight he didn't understand. Didn't want to. He looked into her eyes, trying to fathom their depths. They glittered like agates. They were steady on his. Persistent.

"Tombstone's a rough town."

"I know. All of the gringo towns are rough. And they do not grow enough flowers. I want to be with you, Jack Blood. You are all that is left of my father. You were his friend. I am his daughter, but I did not know him. Please. Let me be close to you.

For a while." Tears misted her eyes. She blinked them away. Her chin quivered.

"Suit yourself," he said roughly, aware of Celeste's eyes on him. He broke away from her, gently pulled himself up into the saddle. A twinge of pain tugged at his leg when he swung it over the cantle.

He waved to the women and Antonio. Stepper felt good under him. He swung north toward his former home, where he would dig his own grave.

*   *   *

Blood finished driving in the crude cross at the head of the mound of stones.

The lettering on it read: JACK BLOOD. Born October 20, 1857. Died May 3, 1882. Killed by Harry Mapes.

There were crosses on the other graves now, too.

He picked up his shirt, wiped his face before putting it back on.

The sun was almost spent for the day, but there was more to do. He raked a cedar broom over all of the tracks he had made. If the marshal showed up today, or soon, he would not find any fresh signs that he had been there. If he thought Jack Blood was dead, that would give him more time. He might tell John Behan, mayor and sheriff of Tombstone, that he could close the wanted file on him. He might.

Blood had cut the cedar branch long enough so that he could drag it behind his horse when he left.

Stepper spooked at the strange object draped over his rump, but soon grew accustomed to the bristly branch as Blood rode him away from the burnt-out remains of what had once been his home. The horse was in good condition, well rested, well fed. He had a lot of bottom to him. It was ironic, Blood thought, that he wouldn't be putting the animal to the test. The ride from Cordwainer's had been slow and tiring. After the exertion of piling stones on the fake grave, he could feel the tugs of pain in the wounds. His right leg was weak, tired. His lower back ached. It felt as if a leaden sack was weighting him down, sapping him of vitality, strength.

He rode to the high ground, trying not to look back, trying to shut out the memories of the last hours of his family's life. In a few minutes, he was glad he had chosen that course, rather than taking the easier way across the flat of his former ranch.

A trail of dust, an eighth of a mile long, drifted up in the air on the road that led to the ranch. The dust hung there like a sorrel mare's tail fanned by a wind, but frozen in the dying rays of the falling sun.

Blood let the cedar broom fall to the ground. He stepped his horse carefully so as not to raise any dust. He rode for cover in the rocks. There, he dismounted and crawled to a vantage point.

The riders were closer. Strung out for that eighth of a mile. A dozen of them at least.

Blood knew who they were, without knowing their names.

Even as he watched, the one in front raised a hand, moved it right and left.

The riders in the rear began to fan out, form an encircling pincer.

The man in front would be the U.S. marshal. Elvis.

The others went by a single name.

Posse!

Chapter Sixteen

Tombstone lay sprawled across the treeless plateau, like a basking Gila in the late afternoon. Spanish bayonets and frayed yucca, a grave or two, a shed, were the only breaks in the monotony until one reached the clutter of clapboards and soddies that marked the town itself. Low hills in the distance scarred the skyline. A single mound at the far end of town, beyond the last shack, furnished the only cover for a man approaching who didn't want to be seen right away.

Blood waited behind the bump on the plateau, a sodden bandanna draped over his forehead.

He sat in Stepper's shade, listening for any alien sound, waiting for the sun to fall behind the far mountains.

He had changed a lot in the three weeks he had been traveling, eluding the posse that dogged his heels.

He had some respect for Elvis, who was almost as good a tracker as he was himself. Almost.

There had been times when Blood was certain that he had lost him, but when he awoke, there was that trail of dust, like a mare's tail, hanging in the sky.

Once he had lost the posse for a week.

He had holed up, letting his flesh knit together, feeling that the danger was over. Rifle shots had startled him out of sleep. Not aimed at him. The posse hunting game. They, too, were hard men, determined, like Elvis, to bring him in.

So, the false grave had not fooled them.

He had watched as they tore it to pieces, like dogs fighting over a single fowl, and heard their whoop when they had found no corpse. That's when he had made tracks out of there. Not toward Benson or Tombstone, but toward the Dragoons, the only haven he was likely to have. And someone in that party knew the Dragoons. They knew where every *tenaje* was, every spring. He had led them to alkali wells and over steep treacherous ridges. He had doubled back on them, circled, ridden their flanks. No rest, little sleep. Just dry food and lizards to eat. He was slimmed down and hard as tempered steel.

Finally, a week ago, he had eluded them.

Luck. Pure luck.

The herd of wild horses had saved his bacon. He had chsed them for miles, staying in their clutter of tracks. Finally, he had scattered them on a sunbaked dry lake bed where the wind swept tracks away as fast a man could make them. There the clay had hardened into stone, the alkali-caked mud had cracked a century ago and each fissure had widened over the years. It was a no-man's land of heat and blistering winds—five miles of hell, where there wasn't a trace of life or the track of man or beast.

Now, he was close to Tombstone, close enough to ride in under cover of darkness and slip into a new identity. His beard was thick on his face, his face

leaner than before. His wounds were nearly fully
healed, the pink new flesh now taking on the color-
ation of his skin, rising in darker-colored bumps
out of the bullet holes.

Hunger gnawed at his innards. Stepper was showing rib bones, his flanks caved in from lack of grain.
His coat was shabby, caked with mud, dust, alkali
and bleeding from blow flies. A sorry sight, the both
of them. Blood's eyes were red-rimmed, scratched
by wind and fine dust, weary from lack of sleep. Yet
one thought had kept him going, given him strength.

Get Jubal!

And, after Jubal, Mapes and Cooper.

The sun had been hot all day, but the western
sky was already darkening with furled clouds blowing in from the northwest. The dawn had been
blood red and all day the wind had been circling,
sniffing at his back, then blowing into his face.
Strong gusts had peppered his face with fine grit,
stung his face and eyes. Now, the promise of the red
morning was in the ominous sunset building west
of the town. There would be rain before morning—a
frog-strangler unless he missed his guess—maybe
even before he left the safety of the hill and started
into town.

The wind freshened and he felt the change. The
chill in the air. The dampness. He took the bandanna from his forehead, squeezed the moisture
out. Stepper bristled, perked his ears. His nostrils
flared as he sniffed the quick gust of wind that
fanned his mane from the northwest.

Red sky at morning.

He knew the sailor's term.

Take warning.

Rains came sudden to that arid land, he knew.

Flash floods had washed many a rider into the grave, many a horse, many a beef.

He stood up, marked the sun's position. He held up a pair of fingers, aligned them horizontally between the sun and the horizon. One finger was enough. Less than fifteen minutes before sunset. A fluttering in his stomach. A feather scraping across the back of his neck. A razor sawing across the nerves in his brain.

Soon he would be in Tombstone.

That's where the danger was.

But that's where Jubal might be too.

Mapes and Cooper, as well.

The killers of his wife and son. Killers of Tío Carlos.

Killers he would kill.

He caught up Stepper's reins. "Come on, boy. Let's get to it."

Blood swung into the saddle, circled the small hill and headed for Tombstone. The sun was down, buried beyond the clouds, the far mountains. The shadows deepened, the lights winked on in the town. Blood rode slowly, letting the darkness deepen.

He heard horses, the low talk of men: miners riding down out of the hills to slake their thirsts, seek the company of painted women; ranchers coming into town to swap lies at a saloon or sit at the tables bucking the tiger at faro, or playing three-card monte, poker, at places where the law looked the other way.

At Fifth and Tough Nut, he pulled up to Russ House, dismounted and wrapped the reins around the hitch rail. He went inside, boots muffled on the carpet in the lobby. The clerk looked up, frowned. Men and women looked out from behind rattling sheets of newsprint on the *Epitaph* and *Nugget*, sniffing the stranger out. Blood ignored them. He heard footsteps on the stairs, coming down.

"I'd like a room," he told the clerk. "A week rate if I can get it. Point me to a bath while you're at it."

"Bath's down the hall. One ahead of you. Seven dollars for the room, in advance. Bath's two bits."

The clerk opened the register, shoved it at Blood.

The man came down the stairs, saw Blood and grinned. He walked over to the desk. Blood saw him. Recognition flooded his features.

"Why, hello there, Mister. . . ." the young man blurted before Blood cut him off.

"Hal!" he said, "Hal Nevers."

"Say, you better—"

"Hal, what're you doing here?" Blood asked, annoyed. He pushed money across the desk at the clerk, who was watching the exchange with a puzzled look on his face.

"Me? I'm working in the mines, but you? . . ."

"Just come into town. Been south, across the border, chasing longhorns."

Bewildered, Hal looked at the clerk and at Blood.

"Roy Brown, this here's—" Hal said.

"R. W. Shepp," Blood said coldly. "Out of Yuma."

"Shepp?" Hal looked at Blood in puzzlement. Then, seeing the cold look in Blood's eyes, nodded. "Oh, yeah. R. W. Forgot your handle for a speck there."

"Good to see you, Nevers. Come on up to my room and we'll chew some fat."

The clerk wrote something down on his ledger and turned to the cubbyholes for a key.

"Room twelve," he said. "Upstairs, right."

Blood took the key, muscled Hal Nevers in front of him, up the stairs.

Inside the room, Blood faced his former employee.

"Sorry, Hal, I had to ride over you down there. But I'm going by the name of Shepp for a time."

"I didn't think, Mister Blood. But you're smart. You're wanted by the law here. You didn't—"

"No. Someone else killed Ginny and little Jesse. And old Tío Carlos, too."

"Sorry, sir."

"Be pleased if you wouldn't give me away, Hal. Now you run along. I got to get settled in, put my horse up."

"I won't say nothin'," said Hal, as if glad to be part of the conspiracy. He looked as if he wanted to say something else, but Blood ushered him out too fast.

Blood looked around the room. It was better than the fifteen-cent-a-night fleabags on Allen Street. It had a wooden bed, a high-boy, a sideboard with a wash basin, pitcher, and two glasses, a table and a couple of chairs. Faded prints hung crookedly on the walls. There were two wall lamps and one on the table. He struck a match, lit it, turning down the wick. The window overlooked Tough Nut Street. It was quiet on the street.

An hour later, after putting up his horse at the livery stable and taking a bath, shaving off a month's beard, except for the moustache, he dropped his key off at the desk. Roy Brown, the clerk, looked up over rimless spectacles and blinked.

"Oh, Mister Shepp, it's you. You got a message. I plumb forgot about it when you checked in."

Brown rummaged around in the papers behind the counter, came up with a small sealed envelope.

"Lady said to give it to you when you checked in. But that was several days back."

"Thanks," said Blood, taking the envelope. The

clerk stared at him, neck craning, but Blood didn't open it. Instead, he folded it, stuck it in his belt.

Blood had one pair of serviceable trousers in his bedroll and a shirt that wasn't worn clean through, but both fit him loosely and he knew he'd have to find new duds in the morning. For now, the clothes gave him a nondescript look, an anonymity that suited him. The money from the cattle sale would tide him over for a long while, so he wasn't worried about surviving in Tombstone. He knew the town well, but it was still growing. He had watched it grow from a tent city to a clapboard town, and now it glittered with fancy restaurants and hotels, respectable businesses. Underneath, though, it was still a tough town, proud of its mean reputation ever since the Eastern papers and magazines had exploited the shoot-out at the O.K. Corral, in October, two years before.

He walked down Fifth Street to Allen, the roughest street in Tombstone. Gunfire erupted as brawls broke out. Hoarse yells could be heard, coming from the dance halls and saloons that flourished after the commercial district closed down for the day. The town itself boasted that Allen Street furnished "a dead man for breakfast every morning." Blood was not yet ready to show his face in the Tivoli or the Capitol. First, there was a man he wanted to see. The only friend he knew he could count on in Tombstone.

The dim-lit Tecolote Cantina was set back off the street. A faded sign hung at right angles to the false front featuring a large picture of an owl under the name. Blood went inside, sweeping the large single room with a glance. A man plucked a guitar in one corner. A few Mexicans sat at the bar, begrimed, sipping *mezcal* and *cerveza*. The barkeep looked up, looked down, then looked up again.

"Jorge," Blood said. *"¿Qué tal, hombre?"*

Jorge Sanchez grinned wide, tossed down his towel and limped around the bar. He pumped Blood's hand, shaking it. Then, he looked around furtively, and led the tall man to an empty table next to a wall decorated with a faded bullfight poster.

"You should not be here, *amigo*," he whispered. "Not in Tombstone. It is not true what they say, but there are many men looking for you."

Quickly, Blood told him that he was going under the name of R.W. Shepp and why he was in Tombstone. He told him about the murder of his family and his friend, Carlos Avila. Jorge listened intently, his brown eyes fixed on Blood's face. Jorge was a short, barrel-shaped man, with a wooden leg. His eyes were wide-set, his nose bulbous in a moon face. Black hair cut short glistened under a felt hat.

"I am looking for a man named Monte Jubal," said Blood, "and two others. One is named Mapes, the other is called Cooper."

"This Jubal. I know him. He is found at the Golden Bull these days—now that he has much money. He lives at the Lone Wolf when he is in town. I do not know this Mapes, nor the other man."

"The Golden Bull?"

"It is a new place. It is near Fourth on Allen Street."

"You are doing well, Jorge?"

"Thanks to you. The cantina is my life. And my daughter's."

"Teresa? She must be—"

"She has eighteeen years now. She is in back, making the tortillas, cooking the beans. I know what it is to lose a woman. But Teresa has done her best to take care of this old man."

Jorge had worked for Blood three years ago. He was a good *vaquero*, but a bad fall had splintered the bones in his leg. The leg had threatened to turn gangrenous when Blood had cut it off, saving the man's life. He had staked Jorge to the cantina. Teresa had been fifteen then. He didn't remember her well. Long legs and dark eyes, black hair. Shy. Jorge had since repaid Blood. They were friends.

"I'll have some grub," Blood said, "and I'll ask a favor."

"Anything," he said.

Blood asked for pencil and paper. Jorge produced both, and Blood started drawing a picture, writing down numbers. Both men were absorbed in the drawing and Blood's explanation when a shadow fell across the table.

Blood looked up.

"Teresa?" he said.

"I am Teresa," she answered. "And who are you?"

She was beautiful. The eyes had softened, the skin taken on an olive sheen. Her nose was straight, aquiline, her lips full. Her modest dress could not conceal the sculptured curves, the woman's bosom that fought the bodice. She smelled of mashed corn and wild prairie flowers, of earth and scented soap, delicate perfume.

"Call me Shepp," he said.

She drew back, puzzled.

Jorge slapped her rump.

"It is my old friend, Jack," he whispered. "Jack Blood."

Teresa's eyes widened. She gave a squeal of delight and threw her arms around him, nearly knocking him over. Her lips grazed his and breasts mashed into his chest.

"Little Teresa," he laughed. "You have grown."

Chapter Seventeen

Curly Adams threw the ring down on the table. Jubal looked up at him, saw the look of anger on the baldheaded man's face.

"You got something stuck in your craw, Curly?"

"She laughed at me. The bitch laughed at me when I asked her to marry up with me. I showed her the ring, and she said to come back when I got one with a bigger stone. The damned thing's no-account!"

Jubal grinned.

"Hell, you want to sell it back to me, Curly?"

"Damned right! It's bad luck!"

Jubal frowned.

"I'll give you ten dollars for it."

"Twenty."

"Fifteen."

"Hell, fifteen, then, Jubal. Take it!"

Jubal shelled out fifteen dollars in paper, picked up the ring. The Lone Wolf was quiet, and Jubal was dressed to go out on the town. He wore black pin-striped trousers, a new white shirt, fancy kid boots. He picked up the ring, which was now attached to a cheap imitation gold chain. He put the chain around his neck.

"I know a gal might take this, by and by," Jubal said. "Seen Mapes around?"

"He's waitin' for you at the Golden Bull. Ed Collins is looking all over for you, too. He's got some news."

"About Blood?"

Curly nodded. He stuffed the bills in his pocket, waved to the barkeep for a drink.

"He say anything?" Jubal pressed.

"No. Said he wanted to see you, is all."

"I don't like it. Things've been going real good and now Emm ... Ed's got his tail up about something."

"Whisky," said Curly to the barkeep who had come over. "A bottle."

Jubal rose from the table.

"Don't let a gal throw you, Curly. There's plenty of flowers on the prairie. You're still sober in an hour, I'll be at the Bull."

* * *

The Golden Bull boasted a gaudy front with a billboard proclaiming April Raines as the "singing thrush of Tombstone" appearing in the Arena Theatre, along with "a bevy of dancing girls and a city orchestra."

Jubal shoved through the batwing doors, swaggering with the confidence of hard money and two drinks already under his belt. He held a good cigar in his left hand, the ash a half-inch long. The ring glistened in the light from lamps set on wall hooks and a candled chandelier. The saloon was full, a line of men waiting to enter the Arena Theatre, which was a roped-off section at the rear, with an orchestra platform and a curtained stage. The curtain was painted with advertisements.

Mapes waved to him from a table in the center of the room.

Jubal cleared a path in front of him.

Ed Collins put a hand on his arm, materializing out of a knot of men.

"Jubal," he said. "Been lookin' for you."

"Set with me and Harry, Ed."

Jubal looked at the back of Ed's hand. It was tattooed with the initials E. C. It was stupid, that tattoo. It was why Emmett Cooper had to use the name of Ed Collins—or any other name with the same initials.

Collins took his hand away from Jubal's arm, followed him to the table, where Mapes sat waiting.

"What's this all about?" Jubal asked when he sat down. Mapes and Collins both wore long looks. Jubal flicked his ash on the tabletop and sucked deep on the cigar.

"Been talking to a deputy U.S. marshal, name of Ken Elvis. He's been tracking Blood all over Cochise County and up in the Dragoons. He gave his report to Sheriff Behan and I was in on it."

Jubal poured a drink from Mapes's bottle into one of the empty glasses on the table. His head was wreathed in cigar smoke.

"Get to it, Collins," he said.

"Blood's in Tombstone."

"Huh?" Jubal's mouth dropped open like the seat flap of a pair of long johns. "Where?"

Collins shrugged, looked around as if expecting to see the man materialize at any moment.

"Elvis doesn't know. He kept on after the posse give up and said he'd bet pesos to peanuts, Blood is in Tombstone. Found his tracks on that hill outside of town just after dusk."

"Shit," said Jubal, putting the cigar down, reaching in his pocket for a match to chew on. "You ask around, Collins?"

"I got to watch it, Jubal. Something about that Elvis. He don't look right to me. Man's like a bulldog. Hangs on. Looks right through you. I don't know, he wonders why I ask so many questions. I had to pull back. Behan, he's in a fit. Said he don't want any more trouble. The Earps are giving him stomach pains and ass pains."

"Behan's a pain," observed Mapes, who had kept silent until now.

Jubal looked at Mapes, bit down on the matchstick.

"Mapes, you messed up."

"Dammit, Jubal, he shoulda been dead. I thought sure as Christ he was dead."

"Yeah, well he ain't. He's here and he's huntin' us."

"I better get some help, I think." Mapes turned as the orchestra tuned up. The hum of voices got louder as patrons ordered drinks, spoke of the show about to begin on stage.

"Who you got in mind?" asked Collins/Cooper.

"Pateman and Boggs," said Mapes. "They're in town, hungry."

"Good," said Jubal. "Floyd is fast. Stubby Boggs will back him up. You got any of them flyers on you, Collins?"

Collins took a sheaf of papers from his coat pocket. Each had a crude likeness of Jack Blood drawn on them. A copy of the drawing that appeared in a *Nugget* story about Blood murdering his family. A story planted by Collins.

"Give them these," said Jubal, taking a couple of

the flyers. "And tell them to shoot the sonofabitch down if he shows his face."

"How much?" asked Mapes.

"Whatever they ask. Fifty, a hundred. Besides the reward."

"It's gone up to five hundred," said Collins. "One other thing, Jubal."

"Yeah?"

"That deputy marshal, Elvis. He asked about you, too. Thinks you're in with Curly Bill. Those people on the stage died. The Cordwainers were friends of Blood's. They, or one of 'em, tagged you and Curly."

Mapes let out a breath of relief.

"You're just full of good news, ain't you, Collins?" sneered Jubal, grinding down on the match with his teeth.

Collins got up from the table.

"Best we don't meet for a while," he said, looking around the room again. "You know where to reach me. And, Jubal, was I you, I'd get rid of that ring. It's going to get you hanged, you're not right careful."

"Fuck you, Collins," said Jubal, his eyes gone cold.

"Don't look now, Jubal," said Collins, flicking his thumb toward the bar, "but there's Elvis. The tall thin jasper with the moustache."

Collins walked away, leaving Jubal and Mapes staring at Marshal Elvis. The man hadn't been there before, Jubal knew. He had been looking at that very spot not ten seconds before. Nor had he seen the man come in the saloon. He was like a ghost.

"Relax," said Mapes. "He doesn't know what you look like, Jubal."

Jubal's eyes narrowed to puffy slits.

"No, Harry. And I don't want him to. He's got to be put down."

"Who's the Mex gal with him, I wonder," said Mapes.

"Who cares, Harry. Get to it. I want him down tonight."

"Mapes paled, finished his whisky.

He didn't like it. He didn't like it a damned bit.

* * *

"I don't see him here," said Avril Avila, looking around the room.

"He's damn sure in town, and I aim to flush him out," said Elvis.

She looked up at the deputy with fluttering eyes.

"And am I the bait?" she asked, a sarcastic edge to her voice.

"You've been acting mighty peculiar, showing up here all alone ... asking questions. I figure you know something or you wouldn't be so persistent."

"You're a very smart man, Sheriff."

"Marshal," said Elvis stiffly. Avril had been walking the street, going into places where she had no business going when he had spotted her. Some backtracking had revealed that she had been in Tombstone for three days, asking about the man whose drawing appeared on the poster printed by the *Epitaph,* owned by John Clum. It was the only likeness of the man he was hunting. The curious part was that the Mexican girl, Miss Avila, was asking for a man that fit the description of Jack Blood but the name she used was Shepp.

"You going to tell me who this Shepp feller is?" he asked.

"A friend of mine."

"Is he hiding out Blood?"

Avril suppressed a smile.

"Maybe," she said coyly.

Exasperated, Elvis started to say something when the orchestra struck up a lively overture. Applause deafened him, drowned the first word out of his mouth.

The curtains slowly opened as the orchestra slid into a theme. A tall woman glided onstage. Her blonde hair cascaded down her back. Threaded with sequins, it caught the candlelight and scintillated. Her eyes were very dark, her lips full, red as cherries. She sang, full-throated, projecting her voice over the now-hushed room. She strolled to the footlights in a flowing organdy gown. She sang to each man in the room, a ballad of heartache and broken love that brought tears to some of the more homesick of the miners.

"Who is she?" Avril whispered.

"April Raines," said Elvis. "She owns the place."

"April. . . . Why that's my name in English."

"So it is," said Elvis, his eyes never leaving the ample bosom of April Raines.

Avril started to drift away from the bar. She saw that the deputy marshal was rapt in his appreciation of the talents of Miss Raines.

Out of the corner of his eye he saw her move.

Avril ran.

"Hey, wait a minute!" Elvis shouted.

The girl didn't stop. She ran into a grizzled-faced miner, nearly bowling him over. The man slowed her down. Elvis grabbed her arm. Angry stares and loud whispers arose from the small knot of men nearest the action. Avril whirled and tried to twist free of the marshal's grasp. Men pushed and shoved.

The singer darted angry glances from the stage in the direction of the commotion.

"Leave me alone!" Avril screamed.

Chairs scraped as men rose from tables. The orchestra faltered. April Raines kept singing, raising her voice above the din. A man stood on a table, unsteadily. The table gave way and he fell to the floor with a crash.

Elvis jerked Avril's arm.

A man punched him in the ear.

Howling with rage, Elvis turned to see who had struck him.

Avril saw her chance and took it.

She kicked high and hard. The toe of her shoe rammed into Elvis's groin. He cried out with pain, doubled over in agony.

"You little bitch!" he gasped. His fingers released their grip on Avril's arm. Recovering her balance, she slid between two men and ran zigzag toward the door.

The orchestra stopped playing.

All eyes followed Avril's dash for the batwing doors.

April Raines stood onstage, her hands on her hips, glaring at the fleeing girl.

"Stop her!" yelled Elvis, straightening up. "Stop that girl!"

He started after her.

Men blocked his way. He drew his pistol.

"I'm a deputy United States marshal!" he declared. "Out of my way."

He hammered back, held the pistol pointed up in the air. Men glared at him. He triggered a shot. Men scattered as the smoke blossomed into the air. They cleared a path for Elvis.

Avril ran into a man coming through the door—a bald-headed man.

It was Curly Adams.

She looked up at him.

"Let me by," she hissed. "That man's after me!"

Curly stepped aside. Avril shot through the doors. Twenty paces behind her, Elvis raced headlong, his pistol still in his hand.

Avril ran as fast as she could, the skirt hampering her. She disappeared across the street between two buildings.

Elvis saw her and he saw something else.

A man stepped from the shadows where Avril had disappeared. He carried a double-barreled Greener. He took aim, fired both barrels.

Deputy U.S. Marshal Ken Elvis walked right into a cloud of deadly double-ought buck.

Chapter Eighteen

Blood didn't want a woman, but Teresa Sanchez was there, in his room, and he couldn't refuse her. He tried to, but he couldn't.

"It is no good for a man to grieve too long," she soothed. "It digs him out inside, makes him hollow. Look at my father. Look at all the widow-men. I have tried to get my father to take another wife, but he won't. He grieves for my mother and he thinks that his one leg prevents him from being a whole man. It is not true. There are women who would love him, who would give him anything he wanted."

"Teresa, I'm not your father."

"I know, she whispered to him, a slinking, purring thing in his arms. She had followed him here after he'd left El Tecolote. Followed him and tapped on the door, stolen inside before he could utter a word of protest.

And now she was offering him her body.

She stood on tiptoe, brushed his lips with hers.

"I like your moustache. Papa said you never wore a moustache before."

"No."

"I like it. I hope you don't shave it off."

Her breasts rubbed against his chest. He felt their heat, the rubbery nipples hardening like acorns.

She was beautiful in the lampglow.

His loins were on fire.

"Teresa, you've started something. I don't know if I can stop it."

"I don't want you to. It would be cruel. For both of us."

He thought of Celeste and how it had been with her. It had been good. And the others, over the years—the ones Ginny had never known about—the women, all of them, good; now forgotten, buried, like Ginny. He wondered now if he hadn't been so keen on marrying Ginny because he had the roving eye, thought she could settle him down. Make him into a one-woman man. He'd tried. But, there were those times away from her when the manly urges had become too keen and he had succumbed to the passionate embraces of other women. Now it didn't matter. Ginny was gone. He might never see Celeste again. It didn't matter, and Teresa was right. It would be cruel to deny themselves this fleeting pleasure.

The ache was there, too, in his loins—two hot stones of pain in the groin.

She reached down, touched him.

"Oooooh," she marveled. "See? The one-eyed one wants me too."

He kissed her savagely then. Squeezed her hard against him. Pushed his bone-hard manhood into the hollow of her thighs, against the plush mound between her legs.

Her tongue slithered into his mouth.

A stab of delicious pain knifed through him. He slipped his own tongue over hers, then into the steaming moistness of her mouth.

It was too late to stop.

He carried her to the bed, her arms around his neck. She was light in his arms. Tiny, dark, wanton.

He lay her down, stood up. Began to peel off his shirt.

She pulled her dress up over her head. It whispered off her body, exposing bare breasts, taut nipples. She slipped out of her panties, kicked her sandals onto the floor. He hung his gunbelt on the corner post of the bed, sat down and tugged off his boots. He peeled out of his trousers, undershorts.

Teresa stared at him with glittering eyes.

She reached out, touched the wound on his leg.

"It's ugly," she husked, "and beautiful. Does it hurt?"

"Not any more."

Her body was golden in the tawny light from the flickering lamp. He eased next to her, took her in his arms. Kissed her. She nestled against him, her flesh warm.

"*¿Tu eres virgen?*" he asked in Spanish. He couldn't bring himself to say it in English.

"No," she said. "My uncle. A long time ago. And a boy who went away and never returned. Does it matter?"

He smiled, hugged her close.

"No. Being first is not important."

"You are a strange man, Jack Blood."

"You talk too damned much," he gruffed, kissing her again.

His hand slid down to a breast, squeezed it gently. His finger taunted the nipple, traced a path over the spongy nubbin.

Teresa winced with a quick shiver of delight.

"Kiss me there. On my breasts," she whispered.

He took her breast in his mouth. Her hand found his hardness, closed around it, tightened so that he nearly came in her hand. He sucked in a deep breath, slid a hand down to her thighs. Cupped the nest-mound. Felt her shiver with a sudden spasm.

"Take me," she husked.

She was ready. He rose above her, sank his hips toward hers.

She grasped his swollen shaft, guided him inside her.

She shuddered as his cock slid into her sheath.

"Oh, oh, oh," she screamed softly. Legs spread wide, she rocked to the rhythm of his thrusts. Orgasmic spasms rippled through her body like summer heat lightning. Her fingernails raked his broad bare back, dug in whenever she climaxed. He plumbed her deep, stroked her slow. Teresa was pure pleasure . . . and forgetfulness.

He could not wipe away the memory of Ginny with a woman. Not one, not several. Nor did he want to. Memories were all man had that were all his own. That no one could take away from him as long as he was breathing. Ginny was Ginny and she had had her place in his life, his past. Teresa was for the moment, the now. The only time that existed for sure. He could not live his past, nor see into the future. There was only this moment of existence and it was enough.

"It is good?" she asked him.

"Very good," he said—and meant it.

"I'm full of you, Jack Blood. You are not angry with me? For being so bold?"

"No, Teresa. If you had not come here. . . ."

"I know. You would not have pursued me. I knew that. I wanted you. I dreamed of you for a long

time, but you belonged to someone else. When I was
growing up, I used to listen to Papa talk about you.
He thinks of you as a hero. After a time, so did I."

"And now?"

"You are *muy simpático. Muy macho.*"

Piropos.

Compliments. High compliments. He kissed her
lips, tasted the faint salt of tears.

"You are crying," he said.

"For happiness only."

He didn't press it. But it seemed to him that she
held onto him more urgently. That she meant more
than she said. He forgot his own loneliness, realiz-
ing that Teresa had been alone, too, for a long time.
Motherless, a crippled father, a horny clutter of
relatives. He knew loneliness from the inside now.
At every turn of the trail he had missed Ginny and
Jesse. Missed them until his heart hurt to think of
them. At times, trying to sleep under the stars,
listening for a footfall or hoofbeat, a sign of his
relentless pursuers, he had thought that Ginny and
Jesse were still alive, waiting for him to return
home. He found himself looking at crimson-smeared
sunset skies and thinking that Ginny would admire
them too.

"Do not think of her now," Teresa said quietly,
jarring him back to the present.

"I'm sorry."

She knew.

He squeezed her tightly, sank deep. Held her
through the shuddering that came. He smothered
her face with quick stinging kisses, attacked her
neck, the fleshy lobes of her ears. She squirmed and
writhed beneath him.

How had she known?

A woman's instinct.

More than that.

She loved him. Had loved him for a long time. Hero worship. There was no harder love than that. Loving from a distance. Unanswered love. One-sided love.

Her body bucked with a series of chain-lightning climaxes.

He felt himself being swept up with her, with the force of her energy. To the summit, the pinnacle of pleasure.

Fingernails scrubbed his back, dug in as she thrashed beneath him.

Her eyes were closed, bronzed by the coppery lamplight. She was lost. Beyond him. Flying high somewhere beyond the room, the town, the land itself.

He flew with her. Caught up to her, passed her, soaring.

His senses jangled. His seed boiled in the pouch and burst in a milky explosion and spattered her womb.

He let out a groan, shuddered.

Teresa shook. Her eyes opened, sparkled in the lampglow. Her fingernails seemed to retract, like a cat's claws.

"Thank you," she breathed.

"My pleasure."

She tried to hold him inside. She clamped her legs around him, thrust her sex upward. Clutched him like a woman drowning.

It was over.

He spilled free of her. Sated, full.

Her hand stroked his brow. He realized they were both damp from sweat. He touched her slick body, grazed a hand over her firm breasts, the tucked-in kernel of her nipples.

"El pequeño muerto," she said.

"Huh?"

"The little death. That's what they say it is. After you have spilled your juices, your milk."

"Yes. It is like that. Like dying. Just a little bit. A good death though." He smiled at her.

"It is the same for a woman. I want you again. I want to die all over and be reborn like this."

He turned to her, wondering if he could come back to life.

The shattering thud of fists pounding on the door jerked Blood to attention. His blood froze.

"Jack! Jack! Let me in! Quick!"

Teresa's startled eyes widened.

It was a woman's voice.

Blood slid out of bed, grabbed up his trousers. He pulled them on, reached for his pistol. Drew it from the holster.

"Who's that?" asked Teresa.

"I don't know," Blood said, but the hackles on the back of his neck rose. There was something familiar about the voice. The door shook on its hinges.

"Open the door! Jack, it's me, Avril Avila!"

"Jesus," Blood muttered, padding barefooted to the door. He glanced back at Teresa who was pulling a sheet up over her nakedness.

He opened the door.

A distraught Avril rushed into the room. Her eyes were wide with fright. She was out of breath, panting. Blood closed the door after checking the hallway. It was empty.

Avril saw Teresa in the bed. "Who are you?" she gasped.

"I am Teresa Sanchez." Teresa sat up in bed, drawing the sheet up to her bare shoulders. "I am a friend of Jack Blood's."

"I see," said Avril testily.

She whirled to confront Blood.

"Something terrible's happened. I almost got killed. I saw a murder. Didn't you get my note? Where have you been? Why is this woman here in your room?"

Blood retreated a step as Avril advanced toward him. The pistol was a useless hunk of metal in his hand. He had no place to put it. The room reeked of lovesweat. Avril was on the verge of hysteria.

"Hold on," he said to her. "Back off a minute and give it to me slow. Who tried to kill you?"

"Oh!" she exclaimed. "It was horrible! Marshal Elvis was chasing me. I ran into this man. He had a gun. He shot the marshal. Killed him, I think."

"You need a drink to calm down. All I have is water."

"Yes, yes, anything."

He shoved his pistol in the holster, poured her a glass of water. She drank it, glaring at Teresa all the while. Blood saw the note on the floor where it had fallen when he'd taken his pants off. He picked it up, turned up the lamp. He read it quickly.

Dear Jack, it read, *I'm staying here at Russ House. Room 6. I have information for you. Please hurry.* It was signed *Avril.*

"I didn't read your note until now," he said. "Sorry."

"If you had, none of this would have happened."

"Tell me about it," he said, leading her to a chair.

Calmly now, Avril told him everything that had happened at the Golden Bull.

"Who was the man who shot Elvis? Do you know him?"

"Yes."

Teresa was looking at Avril with fascination. The sheet had slipped from her chest and she hadn't noticed.

"Who?" asked Blood.

"Mapes. Harry Mapes."

Chapter Nineteen

Blood stood in the shadows between the two buildings. There was still a commotion at the Golden Bull, but many of the gawkers had gone back inside to watch the remainder of the show in the Arena Theatre.

He picked up scraps of conversation.

"The man stood right over yonder, blowed that deppity with both barrels. Square in the face."

"Who done it?"

"Feller name of Blood or Shepp. That one on the poster."

"Elvis said they were one and the same afore he cashed in."

"Dirty skulkin' footpad!"

Blood got the drift. Something Elvis had said before he died had made people think he had murdered the deputy. And, from what Avril had told him, Elvis had already made the connection between Blood and R. W. Shepp, the name he was using. One thing was in his favor. The moustache he now sported altered his appearance enough so that at first glance no one was likely to recognize him—except Jubal. He didn't know about Mapes and Cooper.

The orchestral music floated out on the night air. A woman's voice sang a plaintive song. He could hear some of the words. It was a sad song, sung deep-throated. That would be April Raines, the woman on the billboard out front. She sang well. She knew which songs to sing to the men who flocked to the Golden Bull to hear her. Mostly miners, some cowboys, a few hardcases. She sang of an old flame, a lost love and the wounds carried in a girl's heart.

Blood stepped out of the shadows, mingled with the sparse remnants of the crowd. A few men went inside. Blood stepped with them, as if he was one of their party. Someone shushed them when they walked in and he slid along the wall to look over the crowd at the bar, at the tables and, like him, leaning against the wall, rapt looks on their faces.

April Raines finished the song. Tumultuous applause broke out in the room. Men stood and cheered. Someone threw cut flowers onto the stage. April picked up the bouquet, bowed graciously, and blew a kiss to the cheering audience. Blood found himself applauding with the rest.

There was something vaguely familiar about her. But he couldn't put his finger on it.

The curtains closed and the orchestra went into a lively dance number.

Blood froze as someone grabbed his elbow, squeezed.

He turned, his hand floating above the butt of his pistol, looked into the eyes of Hal Nevers.

"Hello, Mister Blood. Thought that was you. You cut off your beard."

"Jesus, kid," Blood said tightly. "Don't do that too often."

Hal's hand floated away from Blood's elbow, an awkward appendage at the end of his arm.

"Sorry, Mister Blood. But I got to talk to you. It's real important. I mean, Mister Shepp."

Blood cracked a wry smile.

"Shepp or Blood. It's all the same. The cat's out of the bag now. What's on your mind, Hal?"

Nevers looked around furtively. His hands shook. Blood looked at him, puzzled. Something had spooked the lad.

"Come on, I'll buy you a drink," Blood said, heading for the bar.

Blood found an open place at the far end. There was a hallway leading to the back and a closed door marked Office.

"Whisky?" he asked Hal.

Nevers nodded.

"Whisky," Blood told the bartender, whose shirt was dripping with sweat. His apron was begrimed and it was plain that he had been busy all evening like the other two men serving drinks.

Hal's hand shook when he picked up the glass, drank the whisky.

Blood sipped slowly, his eyes flickering as he looked over the crowd before taking an interest in Hal Nevers again.

"Go ahead, Hal, get it off your chest."

"Well, sir," Hal whispered, "you know when I saw you at Russ House you said you didn't . . . didn't do what they say you did and you said someone else did."

"Yeah. A man named Jubal. Monte Jubal."

Hal's face blanched. His eyes blinked.

"Jubal! I wondered. I'm no dummy, Mister Blood. I can put two and two together and come up with four."

"You know Jubal?" Blood leaned on the bar with his elbows, drew closer to Hal.

"Don't know him except by sight. But I been thinkin' a lot since me and Curly come in from Fort Huachuca. He was acting mighty peculiar and just turned on me real quick after we come to Tombstone. Then I seed him with this Jubal. I seen 'em both together a lot lately. And Curly, he don't like to look me in the eye no more."

Blood's jaw hardened. A muscle twitched along the bone.

"Curly and Jubal?" he said.

Hal nodded.

"Go on," said Blood.

"What you said right now, that Jubal done it. Killed your family. That made my stomach turn over. Curly's always talkin' big about bein' hooked up with Ringo or someone and now he's with Jubal. And, he's got plenty of money, but he don't work. So, I figure he told Jubal you was going to be gone that day, the day it happened."

Blood's eyes turned a hard blue.

What Hal had said made sense. Someone would have had to tell Jubal where he ranched, that he would be gone the day Ginny, Jesse, and Carlos were killed. His thoughts went back to that time. Curly had asked a lot of questions. And, two days before they'd made the drive to Fort Huachuca, he had sent Curly in to Benson for supplies. Curly had volunteered. Yet the man had pretended to be his friend. He appeared to be honest.

"Are you sure about Curly and Jubal?" Blood asked.

"They was just in here a while ago. And that other man, too. Mapes."

"Mapes here?"

"He left before Curly got here. Then there was that shooting. I saw the marshal trying to catch that girl, chase her out of here. We heard two blasts from a shotgun and next thing I know there's a dead marshal. Curly and Jubal sat there the whole time. Everybody else rushed out to see what was going on, me included, but those two didn't get up until later."

"Where'd they go?"

"I saw Curly leave. I don't know where that Jubal went."

Blood's eyes swept the room again.

"Mister Blood, that ain't all. I seen Jubal talkin' to a lawman a few times. This lawman is the one spreadin' the word about you bein' a murderer and he asks questions in ever place I go. Shows them fliers with your face on it."

"The lawman got a name?"

"Collins. Ed Collins. He's new in town, they say."

Blood looked at Hal Nevers with new respect.

He put an arm on the youth's shoulder.

"Hal, thanks. You've done me a favor. I'm mighty grateful."

"Was I you, Mister Blood, I'd lay low. You got too many men hunting you."

"You know where I am, Hal. If you run into Curly, or Jubal, or Mapes, come and get me. Fast."

Blood patted him on the back. Hal smiled.

"I surely will, Mister Blood," Hal said, a little too loud.

Someone coughed behind Blood's back. He turned, looked into the face of a short, wizened man with a swamper's broom in his hands, an apron wrapped around faded trousers.

"You," he said to Blood, "please to come with me. Miss Raines wants to see you."

"Who, me?" Blood pointed a finger at his chest.

"Just you," said the swamper, frowning at Hal Nevers.

"You go on," said Hal. "I've got to get some shut-eye. Those mines open up awful early in the mornin'."

Blood paid for the drinks, followed the man with the broom to the door marked Office.

"I'm Ned Culp," said the little man, tapping politely on the office door. "I work for Miss Raines, personal." He talked with a slight impediment. He was typical of men who had fought in the War Between the States and had come out of it without any visible wounds. The noise of battle, the fear, the carnage, had taken something out of them. Such men usually wound up on the public dole or in menial jobs.

"Come in," said a woman's voice.

Ned opened the door.

"Here he is, Miss Raines," said Culp. "Jack Blood."

"Thank you, Ned," said April Raines, rising from behind her desk. "That will be all for now."

"Yes'm. I'll be right outside, case you need me."

Blood suppressed a smile. It seemed that Ned fancied himself the lady's protector and champion.

The door closed behind him and Blood could hear Ned's wheezing breath just beyond it. He took a step forward.

April Raines was even more beautiful close up. Her long blonde hair was natural, now, the sequins having been removed. She wore a green velvet robe, open at the throat. Melonlike breasts protruded partially. Blood gathered she wore nothing but the dressing robe since it clung to her shapely form so tightly.

"So you're Jack Blood," she said, sitting on the edge of the desk. The robe fell away from her legs.

Blood tried to focus on her nut-brown eyes, but the legs dangled tantalizingly over the edge of the desk.

"Maybe," said Blood. "I go by the name of Shepp. R. W. Shepp."

April laughed. A tinkling array of musical notes. Her laugh was infectious.

Blood only smiled.

"I won't call you Shepp. Ned tells me what goes on out there. He heard another man call you Blood. And, I've seen your picture often enough. The moustache won't hide you for long."

"What's the point, Miss Raines?"

"You don't remember me at all, do you?" There was a bitter edge to her tone. "Funny. I thought of you and wondered how it would be when we met again. I imagined that you would take me into your arms and smother me with kisses and tell me how you yearned for me all these years."

Blood looked at her sharply, trying to understand her meaning. He looked around the office, as if trying to find some clue as to why he ought to know her. The flowers that had been thrown up onstage were in a vase. The desk had a quill pen standing next to an inkwell, a few papers, scattered on it, an ashtray full of frayed matchsticks and a cigar butt, a paperweight. The walls had a few prints, Currier & Ives, a photograph or two. Both of these were blurred, faded. Billboard posters adorned two of the walls, both featuring April Raines. Raines. The name was familiar. April was not at all familiar. He would remember a name like that.

"I'm sorry, ma'am. I never knew anybody named April. And the only Raines I know of is clear back in—"

"Bud Raines? He's dead, I'm sorry to say."

"Bud Raines! Yeah. I worked for him once. I was

just a kid. That was back in Ellsworth. You kin to him?"

"I'm his daughter," April said flatly. Her disappointment showed in the dour expression on her face. "Ginny Ware and I used to be close friends until she met you. After that I didn't see her much any more. You went to work for Larrabee at the freight office."

Recognition slowly crept into Blood's consciousness.

"You're Abigail!" he said, grinning.

April shuddered.

"A name I loathe! I changed it to April. For professional reasons."

"How did you come to own this place?"

"Pa came here, struck it rich in silver. Bought the building. Mainly to give me a chance to be what I wanted to be. A singer. He died two years ago and—"

"I'm sorry, Ab . . . April."

"I didn't bring you here to talk about myself," she said, sliding off the desk. She came close to him, appraised him with frank brown eyes. He smelled the heady scent of her perfume, the talc, the womanly musk of her. "It's Ginny. They say you murdered her and you had a little boy, too."

"I didn't murder anyone."

She let out a sigh.

"I believe you," she said. "Even before you walked in here. Unfortunately, a man was killed outside my place tonight and that man was holding a warrant for your arrest. They're saying you shot him because you're on the run."

Blood said nothing. A warning bell was tolling in some subterranean cavern of his brain. A sunken chime that was faint and faraway.

"All right," she said abruptly, turning away. "It's

my turn to say I'm sorry. About Ginny. And your
son. I was jealous of her a long time ago. You
fought over her. Killed Eli Jubal."

"You knew him. He was a hothead. He came
after me. I won't apologize for that. But it wasn't
murder."

The bell got louder.

"Will you let me help you, Jack? I live in the
Harwood house on Fremont. I bought it from Bill
after that shoot-out at the O.K. Corral two years
ago. After Billy Clanton died there, Bill didn't want
to live there any more."

"I know it."

"Come see me. Tonight, if you want. I have one
more short show to do and then—"

"Some other time. Do you know why I came here?"

"No. It was not a very smart thing to do."

"I'm hunting Monte Jubal. He killed Ginny. He
and three other men. One of them is dead. The
others are here in Tombstone, I'm sure. Jubal and
Mapes were here tonight."

"Oh? I haven't seen Monte in years."

The bell clanged.

April Raines was lying. He knew she was. But
why?

"I'll be going now, April. I wish you every success."

She stiffened, then relaxed.

"Please think about my offer. I—I'd love to see
you in private. Talk over old times."

"Maybe I will stop in," he said lamely.

"It's funny how things work out, isn't it?"

"What do you mean?"

"If I had married you, instead of Ginny, I might
be the one lying in a grave now."

He didn't answer. He opened the door. Ned Culp
almost fell in the room. Blood turned, raised a hand.

"Good-bye, April," he said. His eyes went to the ashtray again. Something about those matchsticks bothered him. Triggered a trace of memory. It was there, just out of reach, crawling up the walls of his mind. Something important. Something he had seen somewhere before and couldn't recall for certain.

"I'll be seeing you, Jack," said April as he walked away. "Real soon."

Chapter Twenty

Blood saw no sign of anyone watching Russ House
when he returned. He tiptoed past Avril's room and
opened the door to his own room quietly. Inside, he
locked the door and felt his way to the bed. He did
not light the lamp. Avril had asked him to stop in
when he returned, but he was weary and strangely
keyed up. Teresa, he realized, had made the bed
before she left.

It had been awkward with the two women there.
Avril's accusing eyes, Teresa's embarrassment, his
own.

He had wanted to ask Avril about Celeste, but
that could wait.

He was getting close. Mapes had murdered Elvis
and that told him something. He did Jubal's dirty
work for him.

And Curly Adams—he would have to be added to
the list. If he had told Jubal about the drive to Fort
Huachuca, then he was as much responsible for the
deaths on the ranch as Jubal.

Where would it stop? How would it end?

He slipped off his boots, undressed in the dark. He
hung his gunbelt over the bedstead and crawled under
the covers. Weariness rolled over him. He threw
an arm up over his forehead, stared into the dark.

April Raines. Little Abigail Raines, daughter of
Bud Raines, who used to run cattle on a little spread
outside of Ellsworth. Now she was owner of a saloon in the roughest town north of the border. A
woman scorned. He had never known until now. He
had been so smitten with Ginny that he'd hardly
noticed anyone else.

So what was he doing now? Making up for lost
time?

Blood turned over on his stomach, shut his eyes.
Faint tugs of pain from the all-but-forgotten wounds.

He let the sleep come. Let it overtake him like a
warm sea-tide floating him to a peaceful shore, safe
harbor.

* * *

Jorge Sanchez did not recognize the man in the
blanket poncho, the *serape*, at first.

"Buenos días," Blood grinned. He wore a flat-
crowned Stetson, widebrimmed, with a leather thong
tied under his chin.

"It is you, Blood! And you come to the back door
like a servant. *¿Por que?*"

"I'll walk out the front door if you have what I
asked for. I think I lost my shadow about two blocks
away."

"You were followed?"

"From the moment I left the hotel."

"¡Aii, qué lástima! A friend has to sneak around
to see me. And my ears are ringing with the chatter
of my daughter. She glows, Blood, she shines."

"I will say hello to Teresa when we have finished
our business."

Jorge limped away from the chair, where he sat
on the back porch. He was polishing brass pots with

pumice and water, cleaning out the *olla* to make
fresh *tepache*. The wooden stump left pockmarks in
the dirt. He walked to a small shed on the other
side of the valley, opened the door.

"In there," he said. "I hope it is right."

Blood stepped around him, adjusting his eyes to
the dimness. There, stacked against the wall was
what he was looking for. He picked it up, hefted it,
checked the leather straps. They were strong enough.
The two large chest-sized pieces of iron were con-
nected by the leather straps, sewn together with
thick strips of rawhide. The outfit was heavy. He
set the iron down, took off his hat. Blood slipped the
poncho over his head, put on the sandwich-board
vest. Then he put the poncho on over it.

Jorge looked on in amazement.

"The bullet-proof vest, no?"

"I hope it'll slow 'em down. The men I'm after
like to shoot from ambush. If they go for the head,
I'm out of luck. I'm hoping they'll shoot me in the
back or try for the heart."

Jorge shuddered.

Shafts of sunlight filtered through the shed. Blood
put his hat back on, squared it on his head. He
walked around in a small circle. He was packing at
least thirty extra pounds, but the straps were wide
enough not to dip into his shoulder blades. The
open sides of the poncho allowed his arms and hands
freedom of movement. He made a quick draw. Jorge
hobbled backward, startled.

"Fast," the Mexican said.

"Let's hope fast enough."

It was past noon. Blood had slept late, managed
to leave the hotel without running into Avril. He'd
eaten steak and beans for breakfast at a small café
on Allen Street after shaking the man following

him. Twenty minutes after leaving the Grub Steak, he had seen his shadow again. The man was careless, stupid. Followed him over to Allen, a block behind. He didn't stop the man, because he knew who he was, where to find him.

"I will see Teresa later," Blood told Jorge. "Tell her I said howdy."

"She will be disappointed."

"So will I, Jorge."

The mine whistles blew as Blood walked down Allen toward the Golden Bull. One o'clock. Their echoes died out over the flatlands, rang hauntingly in the low hills.

A block from the Golden Bull, Blood saw the man who had been following him. It was obvious that he had been combing the street, looking for his lost prey. Blood stifled the urge to laugh. The man was still looking and he had no idea he was now being followed himself.

Ned Culp went inside M. Calisher & Son's store. He had just left the Nevada Boot & Shoe Store that featured "Gents Furnishing Goods." By day, Allen Street was a thriving commercial center. It was only at night that its red railroad lanterns were lit and the painted hurdy-gurdy gals plied their wares in the cantinas, the cribs, the saloons and gambling halls that were tucked in between the mercantile stores, lumber companies, and restaurants.

Blood waited for him in the shade of the shingled roof next door. He leaned against a square-cut post under the eaves, building a quirly. He lit it and felt the smoke scratch at his throat, bite into his lungs.

Culp, in dark duster and battered felt hat, came out of Calisher's and hurried to the establishment next door.

Blood fell in step beside him.

The little man looked up. His face drained of blood.

"Just keep on walking, Culp," Blood said. "One wrong move and I'll wring your neck like a chicken."

"Yes, sir," Culp gasped.

"Why are you following me?"

"Wanted to tell you somethin'," he stammered. "I—I didn't mean no harm, honest."

"Spill it." Blood rubbed against Culp's arm, kept him close to the buildings on that side of the street, in the shade. People passing by paid no notice of the two men.

"Heard Mapes talking to a couple of men last night after you went back to the hotel. Nobody pays me much mind. I hear a lot."

"Yeah, Culp. I bet you do. Now what's this about Mapes?"

"You know Stubby Boggs? Floyd Pateman?"

"No."

"They're right handy with six-guns, Mister Blood. In fact, that's their trade. Mapes, he wants to set you up, have those two at your back."

"Why are you telling me this?"

"I know you and Miss Raines are old friends. I keep my ears open. I like Miss Raines. She treats me decent. Mapes means to brace you at the Golden Bull. He's over there now, I reckon, and those other two men are right close. I followed you to Russ House last night. When I come back to the Golden Bull they was there, settin' it all up."

"April know you're telling me this?" Blood stopped and looked at Culp's pinched face as he stopped the man with a hand on his arm.

Culp shook his head.

"All right, Culp. Tell me where these two randies are, what they look like."

"Mapes will be sitting in the center of the room, alone. Boggs and Pateman will be settin' near the front doors, on both sides. They're going to shoot you in the back, mister. You don't stand a chance if'n you go in there."

Blood smiled. He tossed his cigarette down then reached under his poncho, fumbled in his shirt pocket. His hand came out holding a wad of cotton. He broke the wad into two pieces.

"How do they know I'll be at the Golden Bull?"

"They don't. They was going to wait there ever' afternoon 'til you showed up."

Blood stuffed cotten into one ear, then the other.

"Why didn't you just come up and tell me about Mapes this morning?"

"Was going to, but lost you."

Blood smiled.

"I figured you might go on back to the Golden Bull and I'd find you there. You'll be a dead man if you walk in there."

Blood patted the man patronizingly on the shoulder.

"I'm going there now, friend. You go on back there and get out of the way. You tell Mapes I'm coming. I want him to know. I want him to sweat it."

Culp's face paled once again.

"What will I say? He'll know I told you he—"

"Just tell everyone there a man's hunting Mapes and you saw him. Tell them the man's name is Blood."

Culp swallowed hard. His eyes watered. He thought it over, nodded quickly.

Blood saw him waddle into the Bull. He waited

five minutes, then walked slowly across the street
on an angle.

He pushed through the batwing doors, stood there
for a moment, his eyes adjusting to the light.

It was quiet inside. Like a tomb.

Ned Culp stood, white-faced, at the far end of the
bar. The barkeep's hand stopped in midair as he
reached for a glass. Three or four men stood at the
bar, staring at the poncho-clad man who had just
entered.

In the center of the room, Harry Mapes sat, facing
the batwing doors.

On the table, a sawed-off shotgun lay within easy
reach. It was cocked. Harry's hands lay flat on the
tabletop.

Blood glanced around the room.

A man sat on his right in a chair near the wall.
The chair leaned against the wall, but the man's
feet were firmly planted on the floor. He wore a
thin moustache, a battered hat crimped to a peak.
His pistol was tied low on his leg. His hand was less
than six inches away from the butt.

Another man, on his left, leaned against the wall
near the door. He was tall, lean, wore a sombrero.
His pistol, too, was tied down, ran from his thigh to
his knee. His hand floated near the butt of his
plow-handle. His face bristled with a three-day beard.

Blood took a step toward Mapes. His boots crunched
grit under the soles and heels on the hardwood
floor.

A man at the bar cleared his throat.

Mapes stared at him steady.

Neither of the men by the wall moved.

A glass tinkled as someone moved an arm on the
bar.

Blood took another step toward Mapes. His *serape*

whispered against his legs. His arms hung outside, hands visible.

Mapes didn't move.

Blood stood twenty paces away.

"Go for it, Mapes," he said, crouching.

Mapes moved his hands like a card player reaching for chips.

Blood's right hand was a shadow—a bird's shadow streaking, a diving hawk's shadow. He filled his hand, hammered back. The pistol bucked in his hand as Mapes picked up the double-barreled scatter-gun.

Behind him, motion, sound.

His slug burst the flesh in the center of Mapes's chest. His hands twitched and the shotgun clattered onto the table. He half-rose, his face contorted with pain. His hand clawed for his pistol as a blood rose spread across his chest. He drew, somehow, fired pointblank at Blood. A puff of dust rose off the *serape*. Blood jerked with the hard flat pain that crushed his chest.

Two shots boomed behind him.

Sledgehammers clanged into his back, slammed the iron plate against his spine.

Mapes fell across the table, a fist-sized hole in his back. Spreading like red oil on the table, blood pumped over the shotgun. He slid down, eyes frosted with the glaze of death.

Blood staggered and fanned the hammer back on his .44 Remington.

Pain blurred his vision, buckled his knees.

Through the haze of agonizing shoots of pain, he fired at the man closest to him.

Stubby Boggs uttered a short scream as the lead ball ripped into his gut, two inches above his belt buckle.

Floyd Pateman fired at Blood again.

The bullet struck the breastplate, putting a clean hole through the *serape*. Blood shot backward. One knee buckled. With a mighty effort, he thumbed back his hammer, took aim at Pateman. Searing pain shot across his chest, burrowed deep into the ribs, the muscles. He squeezed the trigger as Pateman stepped forward.

Pateman twisted as the bullet drummed into his heart, bursting it like a muskmelon. He danced sideways on rubbery legs, blood pumping in jetting spurts from the hole in his chest.

He crashed to the floor in a bloody heap.

Boggs twitched once, against the wall. One hand clutched the hole in his belly. He glared at Blood with steely glittering eyes. He opened his mouth, but no sound came out.

Blood walked over, kicked his legs out from under him.

Stubby crashed forward onto his face. A widening stain of blood spread from him. He groaned in agony.

Blood stepped over him, smoke curling from the barrel of his pistol.

He walked through the batwing doors, standing straight and tall. His chest burned with fire. His breath came hard.

Behind him, men's voices rose in wonder.

Blood ignored them. He walked down the center of the street toward Fifth. He ejected empty shells, crammed in fresh ones. He holstered his pistol, shook off the pain. His jaw was set tight, though, and his blue eyes sparkled with light.

He wondered if he could make it to Russ House without falling down.

Despite the cotton in his ears, they buzzed with the echoes of the terrible explosions.

Men stared at him, but no one made a move to stop him.

Instead, they shrank away, afraid of the man in the bullet-torn poncho—a man, who by all that was right, ought to be lying dead in a pool of his own blood.

Chapter Twenty-One

Blood walked up the stairs to his room. The desk clerk craned his neck to stare. Whispers drifted up from the lobby. At his door, Blood started to collapse.

His legs gave way. Sweat broke out on his forehead. A wave of dizziness assailed him as he struggled to put the key in the lock. The door wavered as his vision clouded. He got the key in, leaned against the door for support. He turned the key with effort. The door opened.

Blood staggered inside, kicking the door shut.

There was no energy left to lock it.

He fell into a chair, panted for breath.

Pinpoints of pain throbbed in his ribs, in the muscles of his back, in his spine. It felt as if someone had taken a hammer and pounded nails into his flesh, his bones. He shrugged out of the poncho, hefted the bullet-resistant vest from his shoulders. It clanged to the floor. He peeled out of his shirt and touched the painful spots, where the bullets had spanged the vest. He looked at the heavy iron vest, saw the lead smudges where he had taken the hits.

The door opened quietly.

Blood reacted. His hand flew instinctively to his pistol, grasped the butt.

"Jack Blood? It is me, Avril Avila."

He saw her then, as she stepped cautiously inside. She was panting for breath.

"Oh, it's you," he groaned.

"What happened?" Avril shut the door, locked it. She stood there, shaking. Blood had left the key in the lock on the outside.

"I hurt" he said, struggling to his feet. He towered over her.

"Can I help?" Her breathing was labored.

"No." He felt his chest and winced when he touched a tender spot. "There's nothing broken. Just badly bruised."

Her eyes looked in puzzlement at the iron plate on the floor, the red welts on his chest.

"You were shot." It was a flat statement.

"Sort of," he grinned. He walked gingerly to the bed, crawled atop the covers. Avril came over, handed him his key. He tossed it on the bedside table.

"Won't you tell me what happened?" she asked. "I care. You look pale as wax."

Haltingly, he told her what had happened, every heave of his chest a sharp pain through his torso. The vest had absorbed most of the energy of the bullets, but the bruises went deep, he knew. The pain was fierce. For the first time, Blood noticed that Avril was as pale as he was. Her features were drawn, her lips trembling. She listened, then put her face in her hands. She began sobbing.

"What's the matter?" he asked, reaching out to touch her arm.

She sat on the bed next to him. She smelled of olives and garlic, of fresh ground cornmeal and baking tortillas, of red wine and desert flowers.

"I heard that you were killed," she said. "I—I thought you were dead. I rushed over here and the

people downstairs looked as if they had seen a ghost.
Everyone said you were shot several times. Now I
know why they acted so strange when you just
walked out of that saloon and down the street."

"I'm alive. Thanks to that iron vest over there."

"I have some balm that will soothe your hurts,"
said Avril.

"I can't stay here. Once Jubal figures it out, he'll
be bracing me. I want to face him on my own terms,
not his."

She put a finger to his lips.

"Your muscles will turn to stone if you are not
careful. I can help you. Please. Let me do it for
you." Her voice was soft, yet full of assurance, self-
confidence.

Avril Avila was not what he had expected from
her father's description—a convent girl, frail, shy,
polite. Blood looked into her eyes, trying to fathom
what lay beyond the surface of this attractive yet
mysterious Mexican girl. He saw the command in
her eyes, the hawklike determination. In her face,
he saw the hints of her Spanish and Indian ances-
tors, the dark shadows of the Moors, the hammered
copper of the Mayas, the olive shadings of Spain's
pigments. A pair of spitcurls dangled just in front of
her petite ears. She had a proud tilt to her chin, a
strong slant to her shoulders.

"If I had an hour's time to let my muscles—"

"I'll give you an hour. More. But not here. Come
to my room. In a half-hour, everything will be ready."

"Hell, Avril, I've felt worse after being thrown
from a horse. . . ."

"Those bruises will go deep. My balm will soothe
them, make them heal quick."

Before he could speak, she rose from the bed,
snatched his key from the small bedside table and

glided across the room with a rustle of skirts. He
half-rose from the bed. The pain in his back jerked
him back down. She opened the door without looking back. He heard the door lock from the outside.

Avril had locked him inside his room!

He shook his head, muttered, "Crazy woman."

The half-hour seemed interminable. Blood stretched
out, and the pain wasn't so bad if he didn't move.
He listened to every sound, looked at the window. If
he had to, he could leave that way. As the minutes
dragged by, he began to think that Avril had deserted him ... betrayed him. He shook off the
thoughts. A mind alone could fool a man with its
thinking.

Finally, he heard the key in the lock.

Avril came into the room. She wore a robe. He
glimpsed bare flesh as she helped him out of bed.

"Come," she said. "Everything is ready."

"My clothes," he said. "My rifle."

He climbed out of bed, groaning with pain. She
helped him with his rifle, his belongings. She hurried him down the hall to her room. Inside, she
locked the door. He stood there in amazement.

In the center of the room stood a large wooden
tub.

Steam rose above the staves.

"Get your pants and boots off," she said.

"But. . . ."

"Don't argue. The water is very hot. It will be
good for you."

"How? . . ."

"Hurry," she said, her voice low.

He dropped his rifle, bedroll, and saddlebags on
the floor. She helped him with his boots.

He slipped out of his trousers, hung his gunbelt
and holster over a chair. The room was much like

his, slightly larger. Avril had made it her own. There were fresh flowers on the highboy. The room smelled of violets and talc. Incense burned in a saucer. The shades were pulled, the bed was turned down, the sheets sparkling white. Naked, he walked to the tub, climbed in, wincing with pain.

The hot water felt good.

He heard the rustle of cloth as he slipped into the steaming vat.

A moment later, a bronzed girl, the nest between her legs bristling with dark wiry hairs, the breasts firm, pert and uptilted, slipped into the tub with him. She carried a washcloth and a bar of soap.

There was room for both of them. Just barely.

"Avril. . . ."

"Callate," she said softly. "Hush."

He gazed at her in amazement as she soaked the cloth and soaped it, scrubbed him with soothing strokes. The hot water in the cloth warmed the sore spots on his body. She held the cloth to the bruises, let the heat seep through the flesh, the muscles, into the bones. She washed his back, his chest, his face. Then, she washed his legs, kneading his flesh like fresh dough. Her hands lingered in his crotch. He forgot about pain as his manhood responded.

"Avril," he husked, "what in hell are you doing? You didn't learn this in a convent."

"No," she said, the cloth dropping from her hand. She grabbed his swelling penis and pulled it toward her, then slid her hand back down its length. She stroked him, up and down, slowly, sensually. "I was never in a convent. And Carlos was not my father. I was a concubine."

"But Tío Carlos thought . . . he said—"

"He killed my father. A most cruel man, deserving of death. Carlos adopted me, felt responsible.

He put me in a convent, but I paid my way out, bribed the sisters to handle my mail. My own father raped me. Carlos killed him. He was my uncle."

"And all the time—"

"Yes. I did not want to break his heart, but I was not made to live in a convent. I lived with a most generous man. A man who taught me many things. Now be still, Jack Blood. Let me show you that I am a woman and can make you feel good."

He stared at her, dumbfounded.

"Touch me," she said. "Touch my breasts. Put your hands between my legs."

She took his hands, put them on her young breasts. His manhood rose, poked its gleaming crown out of the water at his waist. His hands burned where he touched her breasts. He ached for her now. She slid between his legs, put her arms around his neck. He squeezed her breasts. She kissed him. A stab of desire speared his loins.

Her tongue slid inside his mouth. Her hands played with his black hair. Fingers rattled like tiny claws on the back of his neck. His hand floated down, explored the dark thatch between her legs. She squirmed, rose in the water, and sank onto his rigid shaft. He widened his legs, pushed his knees against the barrel staves. She slid up and down on his hard stalk. He put his arms around her, pushed upward.

It was a sweet agony.

He pumped into her, her body light, floating from the buoyancy of the water. She nibbled his mouth greedily, devoured his earlobes, suckled at his neck. His senses soared. She skewered herself onto his swollen spear, wriggling coquettishly when he was fully sheathed, lingering tantalizingly when the tip of his cock was barely inside the portal of her lips.

Avril was an expert lover.

She bucked with repeated orgasms. Her body shuddered when he was buried deep inside her. She quivered when he slid almost free.

Then, she began rising up and down faster and faster.

"Come," she said. "Spill your milk inside me."

He could not stay the explosion.

He rose with her, his hands sliding to her hips. He pushed down as he thrust upward. He gripped her hard as his seed burst inside her. She clasped him tightly to her until the spasms passed.

She rose out of the tub, a dripping water nymph.

Blood looked at her in awe.

"You're some woman," he said quietly.

"I am not finished with you yet," she said. She stepped out of the tub, took his hand. He followed her. Avril took a towel from a stack on a low table, began rubbing his body dry. "Lie down," she told him, "while I finish drying myself."

He lay on the bed, his body singing with energy. The pinpoints of pain had dulled, were no longer piercing.

Avril slid a table over next to the bed. On it were jars of unguents and balms.

"Turn over," she said. He lay flat on his stomach. Strong delicate hands applied a soothing balm to his back. She turned him over on his back and did the same to his chest. He felt the heat soak into his flesh.

"Sleep," she said. "No one will bother you here."

"What will you do?"

"I will watch over you. I will be your ears, your eyes."

She leaned over, kissed him. Her breasts, the still-hard nipples, brushed his skin.

"I want you again," he said.

"You must rest, now. Later." She drew away. Blood closed his eyes to shut out the image of her golden body shimmering a few feet away—her black hair sleek and shining over her shoulders, her buttocks full and proud, her legs lean and strong.

He fell asleep, wanting her, wanting the mystery of her all over again.

* * *

Blood woke with a start.

The world was shaking, pounding.

The room was dark.

"Quickly. Get dressed," whispered Avril. "They know you are here."

Groggily, Blood sat up, eased out of bed. Avril handed him his clothes. He saw that she was dressed. She picked up a small nickel-plated pistol, a .32 Smith & Wesson.

"Who is it?" she called.

"Open up. I'm Deputy Collins. I have a warrant for the arrest of Jack Blood. We know he's in there."

Blood pulled on his boots, strapped on his pistol.

"Go away!" shouted Avril. "I'm alone!"

"Bullshit, lady. I'll shoot my way in if I have to."

Blood was ready.

"No," said Avril, "you must get away. The window!"

Blood walked over to it. He lifted the shade, looked out onto Fifth Street. The lower roof was just beneath the window. He could jump there, slide down. The drop would be about a dozen feet or so. He could make it.

"Open up or I start shooting this door apart!" Collins said.

"Go!" whispered Avril.

"I'll be at El Tecolote, at the end of Allen Street," Blood told her.

"I know it," she said. "Hurry."

Blood was halfway out the window when the shots rang out. He hesitated, Avril rushed up and pushed him the rest of the way out. His boots hit the slanting roof. He fell on his rump, started sliding. He reached out to grab something, but nothing was there. He went over the edge, dropped to the street in darkness.

It was deserted.

Above him, more shots.

Two of them—at least two—were small caliber.

Chapter Twenty-Two

"It looks very bad for you, *amigo*," said Jorge Sanchez. "John Behan's men are combing the town for you."

Blood's blue eyes dulled with the shadows of memory. It was morning and he had spent a fitful night in Jorge's house. Worrying. Now his fears were confirmed.

"You're telling me that Avril Avila is dead and that they are saying I killed her?"

Jorge nodded solemnly. He sat one-legged on the kitchen chair, his wooden leg unstrapped, leaning against the table. Teresa sat stiffly next to Blood, her eyes wet.

"That can't be true!" she said.

"Who is saying this?" asked Blood.

"A deputy named Ed Collins. He has a Winchester rifle that is yours. He is saying that you shot the girl with that rifle."

"Collins is a liar," Blood said. "You know him?"

"He is new."

"Describe him for me."

"He is a nervous man. He has the light hair that comes to his shoulders. His lips are thin, narrow. He is a young man with pale eyes. He has the spit at the corners of his mouth all the time as if he is rabid."

Blood closed his eyes. He heard Ginny's voice again, describing those who raped her. Describing the man who roped little Jesse, dragged him.

"Anything else?" he said, opening his eyes.

"On his hand, he has the tattoo. The initials of his name. E.C."

"Ed Collins," mused Blood. "Or Emmett Cooper." He got up from the table, paced the floor as Jorge and his daughter stared at him. "It has to be him. He claims I killed Avril. He knows I didn't. He's been dogging my heels. Everywhere I turn, his damned name comes up. Jorge, I need some favors. It's important, but it could be dangerous."

"Anything you ask, my friend."

Blood sat back down, leaned over the table. He spoke earnestly.

"There is a man who works for April Raines at the Golden Bull. Ned Culp. Get a message to him. Tell him I want to talk to April. Here. Day after tomorrow. Eight o'clock in the evening. Sharp. Don't tell April direct. And don't let Culp tell her you gave him the message. Tell him it's important I talk to her. A matter of life and death."

"I will do this. He is the swamper there. I know his face."

"Good. Then I want you to see this Deputy Ed Collins. Tell him you want to buy a piece of jewelry. A wedding ring with a small diamond. Tell him you will pay in gold. If he does not have the ring, then follow him. See where he goes."

"This ring, you know of it?"

"It was Ginny's ring. Either Collins, if that's his name, or Jubal, must have it. Either way, if Collins meets Jubal, I'll know. Be careful. If he does, there will be one more thing you will have to do. I will tell you what I will need once this Collins takes the baited hook. *Ten cuidado, amigo mío,*"

"Don't worry. I will be your eyes and your ears."

Blood grimaced. Those were the same words Avril had used. And now she was dead.

* * *

Spittle bubbled at the corners of Deputy Sheriff Ed Collins's mouth. He blew and sucked at the bubbles until they expanded and contracted. His pale blue eyes were vacuous.

"You've cinched it all right," said Jubal, "but around a damned empty barrel. You let the bastard get away."

"Hell, it was that woman what helped him, Jubal. She singed my hairs with that little nickel-plated widowmaker so's I had to cut her down, cover my tracks."

"So now the reward for Blood has gone up and he's still free. Christ, Mapes had him cold."

"What about Pateman and Boggs?"

"Who'd have thought the bastard would wear an iron vest? He's some sneaky sonofabitch."

"Sneakier'n you think," said Collins, picking up a shredded match that Jubal had discarded. They sat in the Lone Wolf, drinking from a pail of Zang's. Jubal looked like hell, Collins thought. The man's eyes were red-rimmed, his face bloated from drink. He chewed matches one after the other. Well, he had a lot on his mind.

"What's that supposed to mean?" Jubal snarled, cocking his head back as he glared at the erstwhile deputy.

"Had a visitor a few minutes ago, up at the Golden Bull. He wanted to buy a wedding ring."

"Yeah?" Jubal still hadn't gotten it. Collins played him on out with the mental rope, like a calf running with the slack. He'd get jerked when he got to the end of the riata.

"Wanted a particular ring. Small diamond, gold. 'Bout like that one you took off'n Blood's woman."

Jubal exploded in a rage. He shot a hand across the table, grabbed Collins' vest, twisted it in his fist.

"Who, dammit? Who asked you?"

"Don't know. A Mexican. I seen him around."

"You asshole. He's in with Blood." Jubal's teeth ground down on the matchstick in his mouth, splintered it.

"Back off, Jubal. Curly's follerin' the Mexican. He should be back anytime to let me know who he is, where he is. I figger he'll lead us right smack to Blood."

Jubal relaxed his fingers, released his grip on Collins's vest. Collins seemed unruffled, sure of himself. Jubal had changed. He was no longer the cocksure leader he had been. Collins didn't know what had changed him, but he had a few ideas. Blood's killing of Mapes was part of it. But, he suspected, Jubal had another reason for being nervous. He had himself a woman. Collins didn't know who she was yet, but all the signs were there. Jubal was short-tempered, nervous, half-asleep in the day, bright-eyed at night. He had shaved off his rough beard, taken to wearing toilet water. He had bought new clothes, kept his boots shined.

"You and I are the only ones left of the old bunch," Jubal said sourly. He extracted pieces of matchstick from his teeth, took a swallow of beer. He rinsed out his mouth with the brew, spat splinters of wood on the floor. "Curly ain't one of us. In time, he could work out, but he's still green."

"I know. Blood's a thorn in your side. We need to get back to work. I can't stomach John Behan much damned longer."

"You stay clear of Blood, Emmett," said Jubal, forgetting that Emmett Cooper was now Ed Collins. "Just get a line on him and let me take the bastard out. I shoulda done that when we rubbed out his woman and kid."

"Revenge is a funny thing," Collins mused. "Like a two-edged Bowie. You grab it wrong and it can cut you to pieces."

"Don't give me no bunkhouse philosophy, dammit."

The men were interrupted by a shadow in the doorway. Curly came inside the saloon, sweating profusely. He stalked straight to their table.

"Well?" asked Jubal.

Curly Adams sat down, pushed his hat back off his bald head. His pate was slick with sweat.

"I follered that Mexican. He went straight to the Golden Bull after he left you, Ed."

"Huh?" said Collins.

"He braced Ned Culp, said something to him. Ned went straight into Miss Raines's office, blathered something. I follered the Mex." Curly grinned wide. "He owns a little cantina called El Tecolote on the end of Allen. And that's where Blood's holed up. I walked around back to the house part and heard him jawin' with a Mexican gal, the one-legged Mex's daughter."

"Sonofabitch!" exclaimed Jubal. "You done good, Curly."

"And that ain't all, Jubal," Curly smiled. "I went back and worked over Ned Culp pretty good. Found out what the Mex told him."

Curly paused. Jubal leaned forward. Collins eyed him with pale doll's eyes, empty as buttons.

"Get to it, Curly," Jubal growled low.

"Blood wants Miss Raines to meet him at El Tecolote day after tomorrow."

Jubal's eyes blazed. His jaw tightened. The veins in his neck stood out in silent rage.

Suddenly, Collins had the answer to one of his questions about Jubal.

He was sweet on April Raines.

And it looked like Blood was making a play for her.

* * *

Ed Collins shivered in the chill night air.

His horse stomped the ground impatiently. The animal, a roman-nosed bay, did not belong to him, but he had good bottom, sound chest, strong legs. He was one of Jubal's string. Jubal did not know Collins was riding that particular horse.

Collins didn't care. Jubal had lost his punch, and Collins was tired of taking his orders, jumping every time Jubal snapped his fingers. He was loco over the saloon singer and hadn't planned a robbery. That damned Blood had him buffaloed. Well, no more. Even if Jubal had said to keep an eye on Blood, not to kill him, he didn't have to take his orders. He wore the badge. He was in the clear. Besides, there was a way to kill two birds with one fucking chunk of rock.

The lights in El Tecolote winked out across the street.

Collins rode out of the shadows, the horse's hooves muffled in the thick dust of the wide street.

The Mexican had offered gold for the wedding ring.

Blood was back there, hiding out.

He could kill them both, pocket the gold and move up a notch in Behan's eyes, the town's. Blood was a wanted man. Jubal had no claim on him. Not any more. He had slowed down, was moon-eyed over April Raines. He was old.

An hour ago the Mexican had brought a horse in from the livery, tied it out back. Blood's horse, Collins reckoned. The man was getting ready to light a shuck. The horse was a big black gelding, sixteen hands high, at least. Four white stockings. The kind of horse a man like Blood would ride. Well, he wouldn't be needing it any more. Not after Collins did what he had come to do.

He rode between two buildings two doors down from El Tecolote, through the shadows, into the back alley dusted with moonlight. Lamps glowed through the windows of the house in back of the cantina, burnished them to an orange-gold sheen. The coal-black gelding stood under a shed, saddled. The horse whinnied softly.

Collins smiled.

The back door opened.

Jorge Sanchez stepped out, looked in the direction of Blood's horse.

Collins dug spurs into the blunt-nosed bay, drew his pistol.

"*¿Quién es?*" Jorge called out. "Who's there?"

Collins raised his arm, cocked the pistol, took aim. The hammer made a noise as it engaged the sear. Jorge looked in the direction of the sound, eyes wide.

"Who's out there?" he asked in English. "Is that you, Deputy Collins?"

Collins cursed. Jorge Sanchez quickly stepped back inside the doorway. The deputy let his gun arm fall. Something was wrong. He looked around him at the deep shadows, the mass of buildings that now seemed threatening. The lamps in the Sanchez house went out all at once. The alley was plunged into an errie silence.

"Cooper?" a soft voice called behind him.

Collins wheeled, swinging his gun arm.

Something whispered toward him, out of the dark. He heard it hiss, like a snake. A shadowy snake leaped out of the dark. He threw up his arms. His finger squeezed the trigger. The bullet whined off into the night.

The lariat dropped over Collins's shoulders, jerked tight.

"No!" he screamed.

The rope hauled tight, pinning his arms. The pistol dropped from his hand, thunked into the dust. Glittered in the moonlight.

Blood jerked the rope tight, jerked it hard.

"How's it feel, Cooper?" he said, as Cooper flew out of the saddle.

Cooper hit the ground like a sack of meal. His senses jarred on impact.

Blood ran for Stepper, looped the rope around the saddlehorn, pulled himself up. He leaned over, grasped the reins with one hand. Stepper took out the slack, sidling sideways, like the trained cowhorse he was. Blood dug his spurs into the animal's flanks, reined him toward the open space at the edge of Tombstone.

Cooper screamed as his body was jerked like a puppet on the end of the rope.

Blood felt the weight hit the end of the rope. Stepper dug in, gathered speed. Cooper's horse shied, galloped off in the opposite direction. Lamps came on in the Sanchez house once again. The back door opened. Jorge, Teresa, and Sheriff John Behan stepped outside.

"Be right back!" Blood shouted.

Cooper screamed again as his body bounced, twisted, then stretched out straight as Stepper gathered speed.

Blood rode straight into the open country. He pulled Cooper through Spanish bayonets, over rocks, through gritty dust. He looked back over his shoulder, saw the black lump bouncing, twisting, catching on stones, spiny plants. He dragged the man in a wide circle. Cooper no longer screamed as the rope dug into his chest, shutting off his air.

The circle completed, Blood rode back down the alley to Jorge's house back of El Tecolote.

He pulled up in front of a knot of people, dismounted. Stepper kept the rope taut as Blood ran back to the man.

Cooper lay face down in the dirt.

"You're hard on a man, ain't you, Blood?" Behan asked. "I've got a six-gun at your back and you better be right about this man."

Teresa, Jorge, and several deputies crowded around the bound and fallen man.

Blood rammed a boot under Cooper's chest, flipped him over. Teresa held a lantern high. Cooper's face was streaming blood. His shirt and vest were torn. Blood leaked from a dozen wounds, but he was alive. His eyes opened, shuttered in the lamplight.

Blood knelt down, drew his pistol. He cocked it. Held it to Cooper's head.

"Let's hear it straight, Cooper," he said quietly. "Emmett Cooper. All of it. How you murdered my boy, raped my wife."

Spittle bubbled at the corners of Cooper's mouth.

"Yeah, we did it, you bastard. We all fucked your wife. Me and Jubal, Mapes and Larson. Jubal's the onliest one left. You want him real bad, Blood, but you won't get him. He—he's got a pretty little ace in the hole."

"Talk plain," said Blood.

"You don't have all the cards. She—"

The spittle at the corners of Cooper's mouth turned pink. He coughed. A freshet of blood spilled from his lips. His eyes frosted, widened.

"He's dying," said Behan, awestruck. "You dragged him too hard."

Blood stood up, looked at the sheriff with cold blue eyes.

"He's dying the same way Jesse, my son died, Behan. If he wasn't, I'd gut him out right now."

Behan turned away suddenly sick to his stomach.

Teresa took Blood's arm.

Cooper twitched, strangled on the blood that gushed up into his throat. There was a terrible rattling sound in his throat. His breath wheezed, then stopped.

"What about Jubal?" Teresa whispered.

"He'll come," said Blood. "I'll be waiting."

Chapter Twenty-Three

April Raines came to the El Tecolote alone. Blood stood up when she entered the front door. The place was empty, except for Jorge behind the bar.

Blood watched her walk slowly toward him. She wore a flowing cape over the sleek green dress. Her blonde hair tumbled over her shoulders from under the bonnet. Her shiny boots scuffed the dirt and sawdust floor. She carried a small handbag in her hand. A chain hung from her neck, an object pulling on it, hidden from view in the cleavage of her breasts.

"I'm here," she said. "You wanted to see me."

"Yes. It took me a while to figure it out, April. Something I saw in your office. In the ashtray."

"The matches."

Blood nodded. When she first walked in, he hadn't been quite sure. But April was too poised and now she had admitted what he had suspected. Jubal had been there, in her office. He had been there for some time. The chewed up matchsticks. He had seen matches just like them in Ginny's room—their room. They'd been scattered over the floor . . . in the bedsheets. At the time, they hadn't registered. It was only when he saw some just like them in the ashtray that he remembered a habit of Jubal's. One he had had back in Ellsworth.

The man always chewed nervously on unstruck matches.

"Why?" asked Blood.

April sighed, stood there a few paces from Blood.

"I've known Monte Jubal as long as I have you. He's a man. You scorned me in Ellsworth. I hated Ginny. I've hated her all these years."

"Ginny never hated anyone. She never did anyone any harm."

"She took you away from me," April said bitterly.

"You were never in the running, Abby," he said, using her given name.

April winced.

"You've changed, Jack," she said. "There's a hardness, a coldness that wasn't there before."

"True. I can thank Jubal for that. I never killed from hatred before. I never hated like I do now."

Jorge coughed to remind them of his presence.

"Go on back in the house, Jorge," Blood said. "We won't be needing you. The lady's not staying. Are you, Abby?"

Jorge stumped from behind the bar, left by the door that led to the kitchen.

"No," she said. "I'm not staying. I know why you wanted me here. You want Jubal. I can take you to him."

There was something in her voice that warned him. She was too eager, too willing. He stepped quickly up to her, reached for the chain around her neck. He lifted the object from between her breasts.

Ginny's wedding ring dangled on the chain.

Blood's face turned to granite.

He gave a mighty jerk, pulling the chain from April's neck.

She cried out, a hand flew to the back of the neck where the chain had broken.

"Why did you do that?" she whined.

"Don't you know, April? Didn't Jubal tell you? This ring was Ginny's. My wife's. The woman he raped and murdered."

April's eyes went wide. A sob caught in her throat.

"I—I didn't know it was hers. Jack, you've got to believe me. It—it happened so fast. I—I thought you had. . . . I believed the stories. I thought you had murdered your wife. Everybody did. Before I could stop myself, I fell in love with Jubal. He came out of my past, like you. Only he came first."

Blood saw it all now. It was sad. She had believed Jubal. Had fallen in love with him. Now it was too late. She had made the wrong choice. Again.

"Where's Jubal?" he asked, shoving the ring and broken chain in his pants pocket.

April's body shook with sobs. She drew herself up, opened her purse. Blood watched her warily. She pulled out a handkerchief, dabbed at her eyes.

"He—he's at the Golden Bull. I'll take you to him."

"Why? I'm going to kill him, April. And another man."

"Haven't you done enough killing?"

"Not yet."

She turned away from him, started toward the door.

Blood walked to the bar, blew out the lamp. He went to each lamp in the room, blew them out one by one. The room sank into a hazy darkness as April waited by the door.

He knew April was lying. The odds were not good, but he needed every break he could get.

"I can't see you," she said.

"I'm here. You walk outside first. I'll stay close."

"You don't trust me, Jack."

"No."

"Who's the other man?"

"What?"

"The other man you're going to kill."

"Curly Adams." `

Blood was close to her. He felt her stiffen. He pulled two wads of cotten from his shirt pocket, stuffed them in his ears, then nudged her out the door. His right hand hovered near his pistol.

The street was pitch dark. A block away, lamps burned in cantina windows. Further down, there was more light. Shadows bulked large between the deserted buildings. The moon and stars were blotted out by heavy clouds. Another promise of rain that might not come. When he had first come to Tombstone, the clouds had been the same. The air heavy with moisture. But the weather, like man himself, was unpredictable.

A buggy and horse stood at the hitchrail.

April started toward it. Blood stuck close to her. His eyes darted everywhere. It was quiet.

Too quiet.

Before she reached the buggy, April stopped. Blood heard a soft thudding sound.

"I—I dropped my purse," she said, bending over.

Blood knew he was exposed now.

"Have you got a match? I can't see it."

So that was how it was going to be. He was ready. Let them come.

He fingered a match from his vest pocket. He struck it on his tight trousers just under his buttocks.

The match flared into flame.

Blood tossed the match into the air, shoved April face down in the dirt. He threw himself headlong atop her.

The night exploded.

A bullet whistled over Blood's head.

He marked the spot where the orange flame burned a hole in the fabric of night.

His pistol bucked in his hand. Once. Twice.

A cry came from between the two buildings across the street.

A man staggered into view. It was too dark to see his face.

A pistol dangled from one hand. The other hand clutched his belly.

Blood watched him pitch forward. His hat brim struck the ground, rolled away.

Curly's bald head looked like a tombstone in the darkness.

April moved beneath him.

"Did—did you kill him? . . ." she rasped.

"That was Curly. Where's Jubal hiding?"

"I don't know. I told you he's back—"

"Abby, don't lie to me any more. Cooper said something before he died. He said Jubal had 'a pretty little ace in the hole.' I figure you're that ace he was talking about."

"No!"

Blood got up, jerked her to her feet. His pistol was still in his hand, cocked.

A sound startled Blood.

Jubal wasn't where he'd expected him to be. It was worse than he thought.

The shot came quick. Deafening. Orange flame blinded him. Powder stung his face.

Jubal rose up in the buggy, fired straight down at Blood. April twitched, grunted.

"You sonofabitch!" Jubal shouted, hammering back for a second shot.

Blood shoved April straight at the buggy, lifted his gun hand. He squeezed the trigger.

The bullet rammed into Jubal's groin. His second shot went off. The bullet fried the air past Blood's cottened ear. Jubal pitched forward off the buggy. April threw out her arms, took his weight. They both went down.

"Jorge!" Blood shouted back at the cantina. "Bring the lantern!"

Jubal cursed, lifted his gun again.

Blood shot him between the eyes.

Jubal's legs kicked out. He staled as his sphincter muscle relaxed. The air was filled with the foul stench of human excrement. Jubal fell back, mouth open in surprise, eyes frozen in a fixed stare. A stare that stretched to eternity.

April moved, crawling over Jubal's dead body.

A lantern bobbled toward Blood. He turned, saw Jorge stumping along as fast as he could. Where was Teresa? He had not seen her in an hour, had thought she was back in the house. But Jorge was alone.

Behind him, Blood heard an ominous click.

He whirled, hammering back instinctively.

Jorge stopped short. The lantern threw a wedge of light over Jubal's legs. April squatted next to him, holding the dead man's pistol. It was aimed straight at Blood's chest.

The pistol wavered in her shaking hands.

"Damn you, Jack!" she hissed. "You always did mess up everything. You ruined my life back in Ellsworth. You've ruined it here."

Her breath came hard.

Jorge stepped closer, cautiously.

The lamplight glistened on fresh blood.

"Abby," Blood said softly, "you just picked the wrong man. Back in Ellsworth, here in Tombstone. I'm damned sorry for you." A dark stain spread

from just below her ribcage, over her diaphragm.
She had caught Jubal's first bullet. A bullet meant
for him.

April's finger coiled around the trigger of Jubal's
pistol.

Blood lifted his own pistol, took aim.

A shout stayed him from pulling the trigger.

"Jack! Don't shoot!"

April looked toward the sound of the voice. So did
Blood.

Teresa and Celeste Cordwainer came running up
from down the dark street. Both were out of breath.

"Don't kill her!" Celeste screamed, her voice quavering with hysteria.

She threw herself at Blood.

April fired point-blank.

But Celeste's momentum shoved him out of the
bullet's path. The lead ball whined past, thunked
into soft wood.

Blood recovered, stalked over to April. He reached
down, snatched the pistol from her hand.

She looked up at him, mouth open, lips wet.

"You're dying, Abby. April. Whatever you call
yourself. I'm sorry for you."

"It—it doesn't hurt," she said. "I thought it would,
but it doesn't. I wanted to take you with me, Jack.
But you cheated me even at that, didn't you?" Her
voice was querulous, not bitter.

Blood shook his head.

"No, April. You cheated yourself. A man forks his
own horse, rides his own trail. A woman too. You
did your own choosing. Take your blame and get
back your dignity while there's still time."

He knelt beside her. Celeste, Teresa, and Jorge
came close, looked at them.

Blood leaned over, kissed April gently on the lips.

"Thanks," she breathed. "Thanks for that, Jack. My beautiful Jack."

A sob rose up in her throat, lodged there. Her breasts heaved as she struggled for the breath that was not there. The breath that would come no more. Blood held her tightly. She shuddered and her eyes closed.

Celeste touched him on one side. Teresa on the other. He shoved his pistol back in its holster. The air smelled of burnt gunpowder, blood, and the foul odor of death.

"She—she loved you, Jack," whimpered Celeste, burrowing into his side.

"I don't know," he said. "Maybe."

He turned away, putting his arms around the two girls. Jorge let the lantern fall to his side. People began pouring into the street, walking up from where the lights winked, attracted by the sound of gunfire.

"We'll have a drink," said Blood, "and we won't talk about this night any more. We won't talk about the past at all."

He felt a squeeze of agreement from the two women.

Inside, he felt something digging into the flesh of his leg. He reached into his pocket, pulled out the chain and the ring.

Ginny's ring.

"Here," he said to Jorge, "keep this for me. I may be back for it someday."

Tears glistened in Celeste's eyes. Teresa realized what Blood was doing and her eyes filled as well.

"You're going away, aren't you?" asked Celeste before they sat down. From the street came the murmur of voices.

"I reckon," said Blood. Jorge took the ring, held it tight in his hand. Then he hobbled over to the bar for a bottle.

"Where will you go?" asked Teresa sadly.

"Where my horse leads me. Where memory doesn't follow like a stray cur."

"But there is no such place," said Celeste. "You'll always be a part of Ginny. And Jesse. They'll always be a part of you."

Glasses clinked. Jorge poured the good whisky, sat down with them. They drank, looking at one another over the tops of the glasses.

Blood knew Celeste was right. He could never outride the memory of what he had had, but there were other things to forget, too. The killing, the bittersweet pangs of revenge. And Abigail—April— the woman who had died out there on the street. A good enough woman who had struggled with her own memories. And lost.

"Listen," said Teresa.

They all heard the crackle of lightning. The windows flashed silver. The boom of thunder followed instantly. Blood took the cotton wads from his ears.

The rains came, spanking against the windows, drumming in the street.

It was a clean good rain, a washing-away rain.

Blood was glad that it had finally come. He drew a deep breath of the moist fresh air.

He smiled at the two women and at Jorge.

They smiled back at him and he knew he was going to be all right. The future was there and it could never be as bad as the past. And this moment was all that there was, after all. He was living in it and the rains had come.

"To the future," he said, raising his glass. "And to the present."

Rain rattled on the tin roof, rattled above the laughter, muffled the tears.